CW00447934

John Burroughs

Under the Maples

John Burroughs

Under the Maples

1st Edition | ISBN: 978-3-75237-661-6

Place of Publication: Frankfurt am Main, Germany

Year of Publication: 2020

Outlook Verlag GmbH, Germany.

UNDER THE MAPLES

BY
JOHN BURROUGHS

PREFACE

It was while sitting in his hay-barn study in the Catskills and looking out upon the maple woods of the old home farm, and under the maples at Riverby, that the most of these essays were written, during the last two years of the author's life. And it was to the familiar haunts near his Hudson River home that his thoughts wistfully turned while wintering in Southern California in 1921. As he pictured in his mind the ice breaking up on the river in the crystalline March days, the return of the birds, the first hepaticas, he longed to be back among them; he was there in spirit, gazing upon the river from the summer-house, or from the veranda of the Nest, or seated at his table in the chestnut-bark Study, or busy with his sap-gathering and sugar-making.

Casting about for a title for this volume, the vision of maple-trees and dripping sap and crisp March days playing constantly before his mind, one day while sorting and shifting the essays for his new book, he suddenly said, "I have it! We'll call it *Under the Maples*!"

His love for the maple, and consequently his pleasure in having hit upon this title, can be gathered from the following fragment found among his miscellaneous notes: "I always feel at home where the sugar maple grows It was paramount in the woods of the old home farm where I grew up. It looks and smells like home. When I bring in a maple stick to put on my fire, I feel like caressing it a little. Its fiber is as white as a lily, and nearly as sweet-scented. It is such a tractable, satisfactory wood to handle—a clean, docile, wholesome tree; burning without snapping or sputtering, easily worked up into stovewood, fine of grain, hard of texture, stately as a forest tree, comely and clean as a shade tree, glorious in autumn, a fountain of coolness in summer, sugar in its veins, gold in its foliage, warmth in its fibers, and health in it the year round."

CLARA BARRUS

The Nest at Riverby
West Park on the Hudson
New York

I

THE FALLING LEAVES

The time of the falling of leaves has come again. Once more in our morning walk we tread upon carpets of gold and crimson, of brown and bronze, woven by the winds or the rains out of these delicate textures while we slept.

How beautifully the leaves grow old! How full of light and color are their last days! There are exceptions, of course. The leaves of most of the fruit-trees fade and wither and fall ingloriously. They bequeath their heritage of color to their fruit. Upon it they lavish the hues which other trees lavish upon their leaves. The pear-tree is often an exception. I have seen pear orchards in October painting a hillside in hues of mingled bronze and gold. And well may the pear-tree do this, it is so chary of color upon its fruit.

But in October what a feast to the eye our woods and groves present! The whole body of the air seems enriched by their calm, slow radiance. They are giving back the light they have been absorbing from the sun all summer.

The carpet of the newly fallen leaves looks so clean and delicate when it first covers the paths and the highways that one almost hesitates to walk upon it. Was it the gallant Raleigh who threw down his cloak for Queen Elizabeth to walk upon? See what a robe the maples have thrown down for you and me to walk upon! How one hesitates to soil it! The summer robes of the groves and the forests—more than robes, a vital part of themselves, the myriad living nets with which they have captured, and through which they have absorbed, the energy of the solar rays. What a change when the leaves are gone, and what a change when they come again! A naked tree may be a dead tree. The dry, inert bark, the rough, wirelike twigs change but little from summer to winter. When the leaves come, what a transformation, what mobility, what sensitiveness, what expression! Ten thousand delicate veined hands reaching forth and waving a greeting to the air and light, making a union and compact with them, like a wedding ceremony. How young the old trees suddenly become! what suppleness and grace invest their branches! The leaves are a touch of immortal youth. As the cambium layer beneath the bark is the girdle of perennial youth, so the leaves are the facial expression of the same quality. The leaves have their day and die, but the last leaf that comes to the branch is as young as the first. The leaves and the blossom and the fruit of the tree come and go, yet they age not; under the magic touch of spring the miracle is repeated over and over.

The maples perhaps undergo the most complete transformation of all the forest trees. Their leaves fairly become luminous, as if they glowed with inward light. In October a maple-tree before your window lights up your room like a great lamp. Even on cloudy days its presence helps to dispel the gloom. The elm, the oak, the beech, possess in a much less degree that quality of luminosity, though certain species of oak at times are rich in shades of red and bronze. The leaves of the trees just named for the most part turn brown before they fall. The great leaves of the sycamore assume a rich tan-color like fine leather.

The spider weaves a net out of her own vitals with which to capture her prey, but the net is not a part of herself as the leaf is a part of the tree. The spider repairs her damaged net, but the tree never repairs its leaves. It may put forth new leaves, but it never essays to patch up the old ones. Every tree has such a superabundance of leaves that a few more or less or a few torn and bruised ones do not seem to matter. When the leaf surface is seriously curtailed, as it often is by some insect pest, or some form of leaf-blight, or by the ravages of a hail-storm, the growth of the tree and the maturing of its fruit is seriously checked. To denude a tree of its foliage three years in succession usually proves fatal. The vitality of the tree declines year by year till death ensues.

To me nothing else about a tree is so remarkable as the extreme delicacy of the mechanism by which it grows and lives, the fine hairlike rootlets at the bottom and the microscopical cells of the leaves at the top. The rootlets absorb the water charged with mineral salts from the soil, and the leaves absorb the sunbeams from the air. So it looks as if the tree were almost made of matter and spirit, like man; the ether with its vibrations, on the one hand, and the earth with its inorganic compounds, on the other—earth salts and sunlight. The sturdy oak, the gigantic sequoia, are each equally finely organized in these parts that take hold upon nature. We call certain plants gross feeders, and in a sense they are; but all are delicate feeders in their mechanism of absorption from the earth and air.

The tree touches the inorganic world at the two finest points of its structure—the rootlets and the leaves. These attack the great crude world of inorganic matter with weapons so fine that only the microscope can fully reveal them to us. The animal world seizes its food in masses little and big, and often gorges itself with it, but the vegetable, through the agency of the solvent power of water, absorbs its nourishment molecule by molecule.

A tree does not live by its big roots—these are mainly for strength and to hold it to the ground. How they grip the rocks, fitting themselves to them, as Lowell says, like molten metal! The tree's life is in the fine hairlike rootlets that spring from the roots. Darwin says those rootlets behave as if they had minute brains in their extremities. They feel their way into the soil; they know the elements the plant wants; some select more lime, others more potash, others more magnesia. The wheat rootlets select more silica to make the stalk; the pea rootlets select more lime: the pea does not need the silica. The individuality of plants and trees in this respect is most remarkable. The cells of each seem to know what particular elements they want from the soil, as of course they do.

The vital activity of the tree goes on at three points—in the leaves, in the rootlets, and in the cambium layer. The activity of the leaf and rootlet furnishes the starchy deposit which forms this generative layer—the milky, mucilaginous girdle of matter between the outer bark and the wood through which the tree grows and increases in size. Generation and regeneration take place through this layer. I have called it the girdle of perpetual youth. It never grows old. It is annually renewed. The heart of the old apple-tree may decay and disappear, indeed the tree may be reduced to a mere shell and many of its branches may die and fall, but the few apples which it still bears attest the fact that its cambium layer, at least over a part of its surface, is still youthful and doing its work. It is this layer that the yellow-bellied woodpecker, known as the sapsucker, drills into and devours, thus drawing directly upon the vitality of the tree. But his ravages are rarely serious. Only in two instances have I seen dead branches on an apple-tree that appeared to be the result of his drilling.

What we call the heart of a tree is in no sense the heart; it has no vital function, but only the mechanical one of strength and support. It adds to the tree's inertia and power to resist storms. The trunk of a tree is like a community where only one generation at a time is engaged in active business, the great mass of the population being retired and adding solidity and permanence to the social organism. The rootlets of a plant or a tree are like the laborers in the field that produce for us the raw material of our food, while the leaves are like our many devices for rendering it edible and nourishing. The rootlets continue their activity in the fall, after the leaves have fallen, and thus gorge the tree with fluid against the needs of the spring. In the growing tree or vine the sap, charged with nourishment, flows down from the top to the roots. In the spring it evidently flows upward, seeking the air through the leaves. Or rather, we may say that the crude sap always flows upward, while the nutritive sap flows downward, thus giving the tree a kind of double circulation.

A tree may be no more beautiful and wonderful when we have come to a knowledge of all its hidden processes, but it certainly is no less so. We do not think of the function of the leaves, nor of the bark, nor of the roots and rootlets, when we gaze upon a noble oak or an elm; we admire it for its form, its sturdiness, or its grace; it is akin to ourselves; it is the work of a vast community of cells like those that build up our own bodies; it is a fountain of living matter rising up out of the earth and splitting up and spreading out at its top in a spray of leaves and flowers; and if we could see its hidden processes we should realize how truly like a fountain it is. While in full leaf a current of water is constantly flowing through it, and flowing upward against gravity. This stream of water is truly its life current; it enters at the rootlets under the ground and escapes at the top through the leaves by a process called transpiration. All the mineral salts with which the tree builds up its woody tissues,—its osseous system, so to speak,—the instruments with which it imprisons and consolidates the carbon which it obtains from the air, are borne in solution in this stream of water. Its function is analogous to that of the rivers which bring the produce and other material to the great cities situated upon their banks. A cloud of invisible vapor rises from the top of every tree and a thousand invisible rills enter it through its myriad hairlike rootlets. The trees are thus conduits in the circuit of the waters from the earth to the clouds. Our own bodies and the bodies of all living things perform a similar function. Life cannot go on without water, but water is not a food; it makes the processes of metabolism possible; assimilation and elimination go on through its agency. Water and air are the two ties between the organic and the inorganic. The function of the one is mainly mechanical, that of the other is mainly chemical.

As the water is drawn in at the roots, it flows out at the top, to which point it rises by capillary attraction and a process called osmosis. Neither of them is a strictly vital process, since both are found in the inorganic world; but they are in the service of what we call a vital principle. Some physicists and biochemists laugh at the idea of a vital principle. Huxley thought we might as well talk about the principle of aqueosity in water. We are the victims of words. The sun does not shoot out beams or rays, though the eye reports such; but it certainly sends forth energy; and it is as certain that there is a new activity in matter—some matter—that we call vital.

Matter behaves in a new manner; builds up new compounds and begets myriads of new forms not found in the inorganic world, till it finally builds up the body and mind of man. Death puts an end to this activity alike in man and tree, and a new kind of activity sets in—a disorganizing activity, still with the aid of water and air and living organisms. It is like the compositor distributing his type after the book is printed. The micro-organisms answer to the compositor, but they are of a different kind from those which build up the body in the first instance. But the living body as a whole, with its complex of coördinating organs and functions—what attended to that? The cells build the parts, but what builds the whole?

How many things we have in common with the trees! The same mysterious gift of life, to begin with; the same primary elements—carbon, nitrogen, oxygen, and so on—in our bodies; and many of the same vital functions—respiration, circulation, absorption, assimilation, reproduction. Protoplasm is the basis of life in both, and the cell is the architect that builds up the bodies of both. Trees are rooted men and men are walking trees. The tree absorbs its earth materials through the minute hairs on its rootlets, called fibrillæ, and the animal body absorbs its nutriment through analogous organs in the intestines, called lacteals.

Whitman's expression "the slumbering and liquid trees" often comes to my mind. They are the words of a poet who sees hidden relations and meanings everywhere. He knows how fluid and adaptive all animate nature is. The trees are wrapped in a kind of slumber in winter, and they are reservoirs of living currents in summer. If all living bodies came originally out of the sea, they brought a big dower of the sea with them. The human body is mainly a few pinches of earth salts held in solution by several gallons of water. The ashes of the living tree bulk small in comparison with the amount of water it holds. Yes, "the slumbering and liquid trees." They awaken from their slumber in the spring, the scales fall from their buds, the fountains within them are unsealed, and they again become streams of living energy, breaking into leaf and bloom and fruit under the magic of the sun's rays.

II

THE PLEASURES OF A NATURALIST

I

How closely every crack and corner of nature is packed with life, especially in our northern temperate zone! I was impressed with this fact when during several June days I was occupied with road-mending on the farm where I was born. To open up the loosely piled and decaying laminated rocks was to open up a little biological and zoölogical museum, so many of our smaller forms of life harbored there. From chipmunks to ants and spiders, animal life flourished. We disturbed the chipmunks in their den a foot and a half or more beneath the loosely piled rocks. There were two of them in a soft, warm nest of dry, shredded maple-leaves. They did not wait to be turned out of doors, but when they heard the racket overhead bolted precipitately. Two living together surprised me, as heretofore I had never known but one in a den. Near them a milk snake had stowed himself away in a crevice, and in the little earthquake which we set up got badly crushed. Two little red-bellied snakes about one foot long had also found harbor there.

The ants rushed about in great consternation when their eggs were suddenly exposed. In fact, there was live natural history under every stone about us. Some children brought me pieces of stone, which they picked up close by, which sheltered a variety of cocoon-building spiders. One small, dark-striped spider was carrying about its ball of eggs, the size of a large pea, attached to the hind part of its body. This became detached, when she seized it eagerly and bore it about held between her legs. Another fragment of stone, the size of one's hand, sheltered the chrysalis of some species of butterfly which was attached to it at its tail. It was surprising to see this enshrouded creature, blind and deaf, wriggle and thrash about as if threatening us with its wrath for invading its sanctuary. One would about as soon expect to see an egg protest.

Thus the naturalist finds his pleasures everywhere. Every solitude to him is peopled. Every morning or evening walk yields him a harvest to eye or ear.

The born naturalist is one of the most lucky men in the world. Winter or summer, rain or shine, at home or abroad, walking or riding, his pleasures are always near at hand. The great book of nature is open before him and he has only to turn the leaves.

A friend sitting on my porch in a hickory rocking-chair the other day was annoyed by one of our small solitary wasps that seemed to want to occupy the chair. It held a small worm in its legs. She would "shoo" it away, only to see it back in a few seconds. I assured her that it did not want to sting her, but that its nest was somewhere in the chair. And, sure enough, as soon as she quieted down, it entered a small opening in the end of one of the chair arms, and deposited its worm, and presently was back with another, and then a third and a fourth; and before the day was done it came with little pellets of mud and sealed up the opening.

II

My morning walk up to the beech wood often brings me new knowledge and new glimpses of nature. This morning I saw a hummingbird taking its bath in the big dewdrops on a small ash-tree. I have seen other birds bathe in the dew or raindrops on tree foliage, but did not before know that the hummer bathed at all.

I also discovered that the webs of the little spiders in the road, when saturated with moisture, as they were from the early fog this morning, exhibit prismatic tints. Every thread of the web was strung with minute spherules of moisture, and they displayed all the tints of the rainbow. In each of them I saw one abutment of a tiny rainbow. When I stepped a pace or two to the other side, I saw the other abutment. Of course I could not see the completed bow in so small an area. These fragments are as unapproachable as the bow in the clouds. I also saw that where a suspended dewdrop becomes a jewel, or displays rainbow tints, you can see only one at a time—to the right or left of you. It also is a fragment of a rainbow. Those persons who report beholding a great display of prismatic effects in the foliage of trees, or in the grass after a shower, are not to be credited. You may see the drops glistening in the sun like glass beads, but they will not exhibit prismatic tints. In only one at a time will you see rainbow tints. Change your position, and you may see another, but never a great display of prismatic tints at one time.

In my walk the other morning I turned over a stone, looking for spiders and ants. These I found, and in addition there were two cells of one of our solitary leaf-cutters, which we as boys called "sweat bees," because they came around us and would alight on our sweaty hands and arms as if in quest of salt, as they probably were. It is about the size of a honey bee, of lighter color, and its abdomen is yellow and very flexible. It carries its pollen on its abdomen and not upon its thighs. These cells were of a greenish-brown color; each of them was like a miniature barrel in which the pollen with the egg of the bee was sealed up. When the egg hatches, the grub finds a loaf of bread at hand for its nourishment. These little barrels were each headed up with a dozen circular bits of leaves cut as with a compass, exactly fitting the cylinder, one upon the other. The wall of the cylinder was made up of oblong cuttings from leaves, about half an inch wide, and three quarters of an inch long, a dozen of them lapped over one another, and fitted together in the most workmanlike manner.

In my boyhood I occasionally saw this bee cutting out her nesting-material. Her mandibles worked like perfect shears. When she had cut out her circular or her oblong patches, she rolled them up, and, holding them between her legs, flew away with them. I have seen her carry them into little openings in old rails, or old posts. About the period of hatching, I do not know.

III

Swallows, in hawking through the air for insects, do not snap their game up as do the true flycatchers. Their mouths are little nets which they drive through the air with the speed of airplanes. A few mornings ago the air was cold, but it contained many gauzy, fuzzy insects from the size of mosquitoes down to gnats. They kept near the ground. I happened to be sitting on the sunny side of a rock and saw the swallows sweep past. One came by within ten feet of me and drove straight on to a very conspicuous insect which disappeared in his open mouth in a flash. How many hundreds or thousands of such insects they must devour each day! Then think of how many insects the flycatchers and warblers and other insect-eating birds must consume in the course of a season!

IV

We little suspect how the woods and wayside places swarm with life. We see little of it unless we watch and wait. The wild creatures are cautious about revealing themselves: their enemies are on the lookout for them. Certain woods at night are alive with flying squirrels which, except for some accident, we never see by day. Then there are the night prowlers—skunks, foxes, coons, minks, and owls—yes, and mice.

The wild mice we rarely see. The little shrew mole, which I know is active at night, I have never seen but once. I once set a trap, called the delusion trap, in the woods by some rocks where I had no reason to suspect there were more mice than elsewhere, and two mornings later it was literally packed full of mice, half a dozen or more.

Turn over a stone in the fields and behold the consternation among the small folk beneath it,—ants, slugs, bugs, worms, spiders,—all objecting to the full light of day, not because their deeds are evil, but because the instinct of self-preservation prompts this course. As I write these sentences, a chipmunk, who has his den in the bank by the roadside near by, is very busy storing up some half-ripe currants which grew on a bush a few yards away. Of course the currants will ferment and rot, but that consideration does not disturb him; the seeds will keep, and they are what he is after. In the early summer, before any of the nuts and grains are ripened, the high cost of living among the lesser rodents is very great, and they resort to all sorts of makeshifts.

V

In regard to this fullness of life in the hidden places of nature, Darwin says as much of the world as a whole:

Well may we affirm that every part of the world is inhabitable. Whether lakes of brine or those subterranean ones hidden beneath volcanic mountains—warm mineral springs—the wide expanse and depth of the ocean, the upper regions of the atmosphere, and even the surface of perpetual snow—all support organic beings.

Never before was there such a lover of natural history as Darwin. In the earth, in the air, in the water, in the rocks, in the sand, in the mud—he scanned the great biological record of the globe as it was never scanned before. During the voyage of the Beagle he shirked no hardships to add to his stores of natural knowledge. He would leave the comfortable ship while it was making its surveys, and make journeys of hundreds of miles on horseback through rough and dangerous regions to glean new facts. Grass and water for his mules, and geology or botany or zoölogy or anthropology for himself, and he was happy. At a great altitude in the Andes the people had shortness of breath which they called "puna," and they ate onions to correct it. Darwin says, with a twinkle in his eye, "For my part I found nothing so good as the fossil shells."

His Beagle voyage is a regular magazine of natural-history knowledge. Was any country ever before so searched and sifted for its biological facts? In lakes and rivers, in swamps, in woods, everywhere his insatiable eye penetrated. One re-reads him always with a different purpose in view. If you happen to be interested in insects, you read him for that; if in birds, you read him for that; if in mammals, in fossils, in reptiles, in volcanoes, in anthropology, you read him with each of these subjects in mind. I recently had in mind the problem of the soaring condor, and I re-read him for that, and, sure enough, he had studied and mastered that subject, too. If you are interested in seeing how the biological characteristics of the two continents, North and South America, agree or contrast with each other, you will find what you wish to know. You will learn that in South America the lightning-bugs and glowworms of many kinds are the same as in North America; that the beetle, or elator, when placed upon its back, snaps itself up in the air and falls upon its feet, as our species does; that the obscene fungus, or *Phallus*, taints the tropical forests, as a similar species at times taints our dooryards and pasture-borders; and that the mud-dauber wasps stuff their clay cells with half-dead spiders for their young, just as in North America. Of course there are new species of animal and plant life, but not many. The influence of environment in modifying species is constantly in his mind.

VI

The naturalist can content himself with a day of little things. If he can read only a word of one syllable in the book of nature, he will make the most of that. I read such a word the other morning when I perceived, when watching a young but fully fledged junco, or snowbird, that its markings Were like those of the vesper sparrow. The young of birds always for a brief period repeat the markings of the birds of the parent stem from which they are an offshoot. Thus, the young of our robins have speckled breasts, betraying their thrush kinship. And the young junco shows, in its striped appearance of breast and back, and the lateral white quills in the tail, its kinship to the grass finch or vesper sparrow. The slate-color soon obliterates most of these signs, but the white quills remain. It has departed from the nesting-habits of its forbears. The vesper sparrow nests upon the ground in the open fields, but the junco chooses a mossy bank or tussock by the roadside, or in the woods, and constructs a very artistic nest of dry grass and hair which is so well hidden that the passer-by seldom detects it.

Another small word I read about certain of the rocks in my native Catskills, a laminated, blue-gray sandstone, that when you have split them open with steel wedges and a big hammer, or blown them up with dynamite, instead of the gray fresh surface of the rock greeting you, it is often a surface of red mud, as if the surface had been enameled or electrotyped with mud. It appears to date from the first muddy day of creation. I have such a one for my doorstone at Woodchuck Lodge. It is amusing to see the sweepers and scrubbers of doorstones fall upon it with soap and hot water, and utterly fail to make any impression upon it. Nowhere else have I seen rocks casehardened with primal mud. The fresh-water origin of the Catskill rocks no doubt in some way accounts for it.

VII

We are all interested students of the weather, but the naturalist studies it for some insight into the laws which govern it. One season I made my reputation as a weather prophet by predicting on the first day of December a very severe winter. It was an easy guess. I saw in Detroit a bird from the far north, a bird I had never before seen, the Bohemian waxwing, or chatterer. It breeds above the Arctic Circle and is common to both hemispheres. I said, When the Arctic birds come down, be sure there is a cold wave behind them. And so it proved.

When the birds fail to give one a hint of the probable character of the coming winter, what reliable signs remain? These remain: When December is marked by sudden and violent extremes of heat and cold, the winter will be broken; the cold will not hold. I have said elsewhere that the hum of the bee in December is the requiem of winter. But when the season is very evenly spaced, the cold slowly and steadily increasing through November and December, no hurry, no violence, then be prepared for a snug winter.

As to wet and dry summers, one can always be guided by the rainfall on the Pacific coast; a shortage on the western coast means an excess on the eastern. For four or five years past California has been short of its rainfall; so much so that quite general alarm is felt over the gradual shrinkage of their stored-up supplies, the dams and reservoirs; and during the summer seasons the parts of New England and New York with which I am acquainted have had very wet seasons—floods in midsummer, and full springs and wells at all times. The droughts have been temporary and local.

We say, "As fickle as the weather," but the meteorological laws are pretty well defined. All signs fail in a drought, and all signs fail in a wet season. At one time the south wind brings no rain, at another time the north and northwest winds do bring rain. The complex of conditions over a continental area of rivers and lakes and mountain-chains is too vast for us to decipher; it inheres in the nature of things. It is one of the potencies and possibilities which matter possesses. We can take no step beyond that.

VIII

There seems to me to be false reasoning in the argument from analogy which William James uses in his lectures on "Human Immortality." The brain, he admits, is the organ of the mind, but may only sustain the relation to it, he says, which the wire sustains to the electric current which it transmits, or which the pipe sustains to the water which it conveys.

Now the source and origin of the electric current is outside the wire that transmits it, and it could sustain no other than a transient relation to any outside material through which it passed. But if we know anything, we know that the human mind or spirit is a vital part of the human body; its source is in the brain and nervous system; hence, it and the organ through which it is manifested are essentially one.

The analogy of the brain to the battery or dynamo in which the current originates is the only logical or permissible one.

IX

Maeterlinck wrote wisely when he said:

> The insect does not belong to our world. The other animals, the plants even, notwithstanding their dumb life, and the great secrets which they cherish, do not seem wholly foreign to us. In spite of all we feel a sort of earthly brotherhood with them.... There is something, on the other hand, about the insect that does not belong to the habits, the ethics, the psychology of our globe. One would be inclined to say that the insect comes from another planet, more monstrous, more energetic, more insane, more atrocious, more infernal than our own.

Certainly more cruel and monstrous than our own. Among the spiders, for instance, the female eats the male and often devours her own young. The scorpion does the same thing. I know of nothing like it among our land animals outside the insect world.

The insects certainly live in a wonderland of which we have little conception. All our powers are tremendously exaggerated in these little people. Their power makes them acquainted with the inner molecular constitution of matter far more intimately than we can attain to by our coarse chemical analysis. Our world is agitated by vibrations, coarse and fine, of which our senses can take in only the slower ones. If they exceed three thousand a second, they become too shrill for our ears. It is thought that the world of sound with the insects begins where ours leaves off. The drums and tubes of insects' ears are very minute. What would to us be a continuous sound is to them a series of separate blows. We begin to hear blows as continuous sounds when they amount to about thirty a second. The house-fly has about four thousand eye-lenses; the cabbage butterfly, and the dragon-fly, about seventeen thousand; and some species of beetles have twenty-five thousand. We cannot begin to think in what an agitated world the insect lives, thrilling and vibrating to a degree that would drive us insane. If we possessed the same microscopic gifts, how would the aspect of the world be changed! We might see a puff of smoke as a flock of small blue butterflies, or hear the hum of a mosquito as the blast of a trumpet. On the other hand, so much that disturbs us must escape the insects, because their senses are too fine to take it in. Doubtless they do not hear the thunder or feel the earthquake.

The insects are much more sensitive to heat and cold than we are, and for reasons. The number of waves in the ether that gives us the sensation of heat is three or four million millions a second. The number of tremors required to produce red light is estimated at four hundred and seventy-four million millions a second, and for the production of violet light, six hundred and ninety-nine million millions a second. No doubt the insects react to all these different degrees of vibration. Those marvelous instruments called antennæ seem to put them in touch with a world of which we are quite oblivious.

X

To how many things our lives have been compared!—to a voyage, with its storms and adverse currents and safe haven at last; to a day with its morning, noon, and night; to the seasons with their spring, summer, autumn, and winter; to a game, a school, a battle.

In one of his addresses to workingmen Huxley compared life to a game of chess. We must learn the names and the values and the moves of each piece, and all the rules of the game if we hope to play it successfully. The chessboard is the world, the pieces are the phenomena of the universe, the rules of the game are what we call the laws of nature. But it may be questioned if the comparison is a happy one. Life is not a game in this sense, a diversion, an aside, or a contest for victory over an opponent, except in isolated episodes now and then. Mastery of chess will not help in the mastery of life. Life is a day's work, a struggle where the forces to be used and the forces to be overcome are much more vague and varied and intangible than are those of the chessboard. Life is coöperation with other lives. We win when we help others to win. I suppose business is more often like a game than is life—your gain is often the other man's loss, and you deliberately aim to outwit your rivals and competitors. But in a sane, normal life there is little that suggests a game of any kind.

We must all have money, or its equivalent. There are the three things—money, goods, labor—and the greatest of these is labor. Labor is the sum of all values. The value of things is the labor it requires to produce or to obtain them. Were gold plentiful and silver scarce, the latter would be the more precious. The men at the plough and the hoe and in the mines of coal and iron stand first. These men win from nature what we all must have, and these things are none of them in the hands or under the guardianship of some one who is trying to keep us from obtaining them, or is aiming to take our aids and resources from us.

The chess simile has only a rhetorical value. The London workingmen to whom Huxley spoke would look around them in vain to find in their problems of life anything akin to a game of chess, or for any fruitful suggestion in the idea. They were probably mechanics, tradesmen, artisans, teamsters, boatmen, painters, and so on, and knew through experience the forces with which they had to deal. But how many persons who succeed in life have any such expert knowledge of the forces and conditions with which they have to deal, as two chess-players have of the pawns and knights and bishops and queens of the chessboard?

Huxley was nearly always impressive and convincing, and there was vastly more logical force in his figures than in those of most writers.

Life may more truly be compared to a river that has its source in a mountain or hillside spring, with its pure and sparking or foaming and noisy youth, then its quieter and stronger and larger volume, and then its placid and gently moving current to the sea. Blessed is the life that is self-purifying, like the moving waters; that lends itself to many noble uses, never breaking out of bonds and becoming a destructive force.

XI

I had a letter the other day from a man who wanted to know why the meadow, or field, mice gnawed or barked the apple-trees when there was a deep coverlid of snow upon the ground. Was it because they found it difficult to get up through the deep, frozen snow to the surface to get seeds to eat? He did not seem to know that meadow mice are not seed-eaters, but that they live on grass and roots and keep well hidden beneath the ground during the day, when there is a deep fall of snow coming up out of their dens and retreats and leading a free holiday life beneath the snow, free from the danger of cats, foxes, owls, and hawks. Life then becomes a sort of picnic. They build new nests on the surface of the ground and form new runways, and disport themselves apparently in a festive mood. The snow is their protection. They bark the trees and take their time. When the snow is gone, their winter picnic is at an end, and they retreat to their dens in the ground and beneath flat stones, and lead once more the life of fear.

XII

Sitting on my porch recently, wrapped in my blanket, recovering from a slight indisposition, I was in a mood to be interested in the everyday aspects of nature before me—in the white and purple lilacs, in the maple-leaves nearly full grown, in the pendent fringe of the yellowish-white bloom of the chestnut and oak, in the new shoots of the grapevines, and so forth. All these things formed only a setting or background for the wild life near by.

The birds are the little people that peep out at me, or pause and regard me curiously in this great temple of trees,—wrens, chippies, robins, bluebirds, catbirds, redstarts, and now and then rarer visitants. A few days earlier, for a moment, a mourning ground warbler suddenly appeared around the corner, on the ground, at the foot of the steps, and glanced hastily up at me. When I arose and looked over the railing, it had gone. Then the speckled Canada warbler came in the lilac bushes and syringa branches and gave me several good views. The bay-breasted warbler was reported in the evergreens up by the stone house, but he failed to report to me here at "The Nest." The female redstart, however, came several times to the gravel walk below me, evidently looking for material to begin her nest. And the wren, the irrepressible house wren, was and is in evidence every few minutes, busy carrying nesting-material into the box on the corner of the veranda. How intense and emphatic she is! And the male, how he throbs and palpitates with song! Yesterday an interloper appeared. He or she climbed the post by the back way, as it were, and hopped out upon the top of the box and paused, as if to see that the coast was clear. He acted as if he felt himself an intruder. Quick as a flash there was a brown streak from the branch of a maple thirty feet away, and the owner of the box was after him. The culprit did not stop to argue the case, but was off, hotly pursued. I must not forget the pair of wood thrushes that are building a nest in a maple fifty or more feet away. How I love to see them on the ground at my feet, every motion and gesture like music to the eye! The head and neck of the male fairly glows, and there is something fine and manly about his speckled breast.

A pair of catbirds have a nest in the barberry bushes at the south end of the house, and are in evidence at all hours. But when the nest is completed, and the laying of eggs begins, they keep out of the public eye as much as possible. From the front of the stage they retreat behind the curtain.

One day as I sat here I heard the song of the olive-backed thrush down in the currant-bushes below me. Instantly I was transported to the deep woods and the trout brooks of my native Catskills. I heard the murmuring water and felt the woodsy coolness of those retreats—such magic hath associative memories! A moment before a yellow-throated vireo sang briefly in the maple, a harsh note; and the oriole with its insistent call added to the disquieting sounds. I have no use for the oriole. He has not one musical note, and in grape time his bill is red, or purple, with the blood of our grapes.

But the most of these little people are my benefactors, and add another ray of sunshine to the May day. I shall not soon forget the spectacle of that rare little warbler peeping around the corner of the porch, like a little fairy, and then vanishing.

The mere studying of the birds, seeking mere knowledge of them, is not enough. You must live with the birds, so to speak; have daily and seasonal associations with them before they come to mean much to you. Then, as they linger about your house or your camp, or as you see them in your walks, they are a part of your life, and help give tone and color to your day.

III

THE FLIGHT OF BIRDS

To what widely different use birds put their power of flight! To the great mass of them it is simply a means of locomotion, of getting from one point to another. A small minority put their wing-power to more ideal uses, as the lark when he claps his wings at heaven's gate, and the ruffed grouse when he drums; even the woodcock has some other use for his wings than to get from one point to another. Listen to his flight song in the April twilight up against the sky.

Our small hawks use their power of flight mainly to catch their prey, as does the swallow skimming the air all day on tireless wing, but some of the other hawks, such as our red-tailed hawk, climb their great spirals apparently with other motives than those which relate to their daily fare. The crow has little other use for his wings than to gad about like a busy politician from one neighborhood to another. In Florida I have seen large flocks of the white ibis performing striking evolutions high up against the sky, evidently expressive of the gay and festive feeling begotten by the mating instinct.

The most beautiful flyer we ever see against our skies is the unsavory buzzard. He is the winged embodiment of grace, ease, and leisure. Judging from appearances alone, he is the most disinterested of all the winged creatures we see. He rides the airy billows as if only to enjoy his mastery over them. He is as calm and unhurried as the orbs in their courses. His great circles and spirals have a kind of astronomic completeness. That all this power of wing and grace of motion should be given to an unclean bird, to a repulsive scavenger, is one of the anomalies of nature. He does not need to hurry or conceal his approach; what he is after cannot flee or hide; he has no enemies; nothing wants him; and he is at peace with all the world.

The great condor of South America, in rising from the ground, always faces the wind. It is often captured by tempting it to gorge itself in a comparatively narrow space. But if a strong enough wind were blowing at such times, it could quickly rise over the barrier. Darwin says he watched a condor high in the air describing its huge circles for six hours without once flapping its wings. He says that, if the bird wished to descend, the wings were for a moment collapsed; and when again expanded, with an altered inclination, the momentum gained by the rapid descent seemed to urge the bird upwards with the even and steady movement of a paper kite. In the case of any bird *soaring*, its motion must be sufficiently rapid for the action of the inclined surface of its body on the atmosphere to counterbalance its gravity. The force to keep up the momentum of a body moving in a horizontal plane in the air (in which there is so little friction) cannot be great, and this force is all that is wanted. The movement of the neck and body of the condor, we must suppose, is sufficient for this. However this may be, it is truly wonderful and beautiful to see so great a bird, hour after hour, without any apparent exertion, wheeling and gliding over mountain and river.

The airplane has a propelling power in its motor, and it shifts its wings to take advantage of the currents. The buzzard and condor do the same thing. They are living airplanes, and their power is so evenly and subtly distributed and applied, that the trick of it escapes the eye. But of course they avail themselves of the lifting power of the air-currents.

All birds know how to use their wings to propel themselves through the air, but the mechanism of the act we may not be able to analyze. I do not know how a butterfly propels itself against a breeze with its quill-less wings, but we know that it does do it. As its wings are neither convex nor concave, like a bird's, one would think that the upward and downward strokes would neutralize each other; but they do not. Strong winds often carry them out over large bodies of water; but such a master flyer as the monarch beats its way back to shore, and, indeed, the monarch habitually flies long distances over salt water when migrating along our seacoast in spring and fall.

At the moment of writing these paragraphs, I saw a hen-hawk flap heavily by, pursued by a kingbird. The air was phenomenally still, not a leaf stirred, and the hawk was compelled to beat his wings vigorously. No soaring now, no mounting heavenward, as I have seen him mount till his petty persecutor grew dizzy with the height and returned to earth. But the next day, with a fairly good breeze blowing, I watched two hawks for many minutes climbing their spiral stairway to the skies, till they became very small objects against the clouds, and not once did they flap their wings! Then one of them turned toward the mountain-top and sailed straight into the face of the wind, till he was probably over his mate or young, when, with half-folded wings, he shot down into the tree-tops like an arrow.

In regard to powers of flight, the birds of the air may be divided into three grand classes: those which use their wings simply to transport themselves from one place to another,—the same use we put our legs to,—those which climb the heavens to attain a wide lookout, either for the pleasure of soaring, or to gain a vantage-point from which to scan a wide territory in search of food or prey, and those which feed as they fly. Most of our common birds are examples of the first class. Our hawks and buzzards are examples of the second class. Swallows, nighthawks, and some sea-birds are examples of the third class. A few of our birds use their wings to gain an elevation from which to deliver their songs—as the larks, and some of the finches; but the robins and the sparrows and the warblers and the woodpeckers are always going somewhere. The hawks and the buzzards are, comparatively speaking, birds of leisure.

Every bird and beast is a master in the use of its own tools and weapons. We who look on from the outside marvel at their skill. Here is the carpenter bumble-bee hovering and darting about the verge-board of my porch-roof as I write this. It darts swiftly this way and that, and now and then pauses in midair, surrounded by a blur of whirring wings, as often does the hummingbird. How it does it, I do not know. I cannot count or distinguish the separate stroke of its wings. At the same time, the chimney swifts sweep by me like black arrows, on wings apparently as stiff as if made of tin or sheet-iron, now beating the air, now sailing. In some way they suggest winged gimlets. How thin and scimitar-like their wings are! They are certainly masters of their own craft.

In general, birds in flight bring the wings as far below the body as they do above it. Note the crow flapping his way through the air. He is a heavy flyer, but can face a pretty strong wind. His wings probably move through an arc of about ninety degrees. The ph[oe]be flies with a peculiar snappy, jerky flight; its relative the kingbird, with a mincing and hovering flight; it tiptoes through the air. The woodpeckers gallop, alternately closing and spreading their wings. The ordinary flight of the goldfinch is a very marked undulatory flight; a section of it, the rise and the fall, would probably measure fifty feet. The bird goes half that distance or more with wings closed. This is the flight the male indulges in within hearing distance of his brooding mate. During the love season he occasionally gives way to an ecstatic flight. This is a level flight, performed on round, open wings, which beat the air vertically. This flight of ecstasy during the song season is common to many of our birds. I have seen even the song sparrow indulge in it, rising fifty feet or more and delivering its simple song with obvious excitement. The idiotic-looking woodcock, inspired by the grand passion, rises upon whistling wings in the early spring twilight, and floats and circles at an altitude of a hundred feet or more, and in rapid smackering and chippering notes unburdens his soul. The song of ecstasy with our meadowlark is delivered in a level flight and is sharp and hurried, both flight and song differing radically from its everyday performance. One thinks of the bobolink as singing almost habitually on the wing. He is the most rollicking and song-drunk of all our singing birds. His season is brief but hilarious. In his level flight he seems to use only the tips of his wings, and we see them always below the level of his back. Our common birds that have no flight-song, so far as I have observed, are the bluebird, the robin, the ph[oe]be, the social sparrow, the tanager, the grosbeak, the pewee, the wood warblers, and most of the ground warblers.

Over thirty years ago a writer on flying-machines had this to say about the flight of sea-gulls: "Sweeping around in circles, occasionally elevating themselves by a few flaps of the wings, they glide down and up the aerial inclines without apparently any effort whatever. But a close observation will show that at every turn the angle of inclination of the wings is changed to meet the new conditions. There is continual movement with power—by the bird it is done instinctively, by our machine only through mechanism obeying a mind not nearly so well instructed."

The albatross will follow a ship at sea, sailing round and round, in a brisk breeze, on unbending wing, only now and then righting itself with a single flap of its great pinions. It literally rides upon the storm.

IV

BIRD INTIMACIES

When, as sometimes happens, I feel an inclination to seek out new lands in my own country, or in other countries, to see what Nature is doing there, and what guise she wears, something prompts me to pause, and after a while to say to myself: "Look a little closer into the nature right at your own door; do a little intensive observation at home, and see what that yields you. The enticement of the far-away is mostly in your imagination; let your eyes and your imagination play once more on the old familiar birds andobjects."

One season in my walks to the woods I was on the lookout for a natural bracket among the tree-branches, to be used in supporting a book-shelf. I did not find it; but one day in a shad-blow tree, within a few feet from the corner of my own house, I found what I was searching for, perfect in every particular —the right angle and the supporting brace, or hypothenuse. It gave me a hint I have not forgotten.

I find that one has only to overcome a little of his obtuseness and indifference and look a little more closely upon the play of wild life about him to realize how much interesting natural history is being enacted every day before his very eyes—in his own garden and dooryard and apple-orchard and vineyard. If one's mind were only alert and sensitive enough to take it all in! Whether one rides or walks or sits under the trees, or loiters about the fields or woods, the play of wild life is going on about him, and, if he happens to be blessed with the seeing eye and the hearing ear, is available for his instruction and entertainment. On every farm in the land a volume of live natural history goes to waste every year because there is no historian to note the happenings.

The drama of wild life goes on more or less behind screens—a screen of leaves or of grass, or of vines, or of tree-trunks, and only the alert and sympathetic eye penetrates it. The keenest of us see only a mere fraction of it. If one saw one tenth of the significant happenings that take place on his few acres of orchard, lawn, and vineyard in the course of the season, or even of a single week, what a harvest he would have! The drama of wild life is played rapidly; the actors are on and off the stage before we fairly know it, and the play shifts to other stages.

I wonder how many of the scores of persons passing along the road between my place and the railway station one early May day became aware that a rare bird incident was being enacted in the trees over their heads. It was the annual *sängerfest* of the goldfinches—one of the prettiest episodes in the lives of any of our birds, a real musical reunion of the goldfinch tribe, apparently a whole township, many hundreds of them, filling scores of the tree-tops along the road and in the groves with a fine, sibilant chorus which the ear refers vaguely to the surrounding tree-tops, but which the eye fails adequately to account for. It comes from everywhere, but from nowhere in particular. The birds sit singly here and there amid the branches, and it is difficult to identify the singers. It is a minor strain, but multitudinous, and fills all the air. The males are just donning their golden uniforms, as if to celebrate the blooming of the dandelions, which, with the elm-trees, afford them their earliest food-supply. While they are singing they are busy cutting out the green germs of the elm flakes, and going down to the ground and tearing open the closed dandelion-heads that have shut up to ripen their seeds, preparatory to their second and ethereal flowering when they become spheres of fragile silver down.

Whether this annual reunion of the goldfinches should be called a dandelion festival, or a new-coat festival, or whether it is to bring the sexes together preliminary to the mating-season, I am at a loss to decide. It usually lasts a week or more, and continues on wet days as well as on fair. It all has a decidedly festive air, like the fête-days of humans. I know of nothing like it among other birds. It is the manifestation of something different from the flocking instinct; it is the social and holiday instinct, bringing the birds together for a brief season, as if in celebration of some special event or purpose. I have observed it in my vicinity every spring for many years, usually in April or early May, and it is the prettiest and most significant bird episode, involving a whole species, known to me.

The goldfinch has many pretty ways. He is one of our most amiable birds. So far as my knowledge goes, he is not capable of one harsh note. His tones are all either joyous or plaintive. In his spring reunions they are joyous. In the peculiar flight-song in which he indulges in the mating season, beating the air vertically with his round, open wings, his tones are fairly ecstatic. His call to his mate when she is brooding, and when he circles about her in that long, billowy flight, the crests of his airy waves being thirty or forty feet apart, calling, "Perchic-o-pee, perchic-o-pee," as if he were saying, "For love of thee, for love of thee," and she calling back, "Yes, dearie; yes, dearie"—his tones at such times express contentment and reassurance.

When any of his natural enemies appear—a hawk, a cat, a jay—his tones are plaintive and appealing. "Pit-y, pit-y!" he cries in sorrow and not in anger.

When with his mate he leads their brood about the August thistles, the young call in a similar tone. When in July the nesting has begun, the female talks the prettiest "baby talk" to her mate as he feeds her. The nest-building rarely begins till thistledown can be had—so literally are all the ways of this darling bird ways of softness and gentleness. The nest is a thick, soft, warm structure, securely fastened in the fork of a maple or an apple-tree.

None of our familiar birds endear themselves to us more than does the bluebird. The first bluebird in the spring is as welcome as the blue sky itself. The season seems softened and tempered as soon as we hear his note and see his warm breast and azure wing. His gentle manners, his soft, appealing voice, not less than his pleasing hues, seem born of the bright and genial skies. He is the spirit of the April days incarnated in a bird. He has the quality of winsomeness, like the violet and the speedwell among the flowers. Not strictly a songster, yet his every note and call is from out the soul of harmony. The bluebird is evidently an offshoot from the thrush family, and without the thrush's gift of song; still his voice affords us much of the same pleasure.

How readily the bluebirds become our friends and neighbors when we offer them suitable nesting-retreats! Bring them something from nature, something with the bark on—a section of a dry beech or maple limb in which the downy woodpecker has excavated his chamber and passed the winter or reared his brood; fasten it in early spring upon the corner of your porch, or on the trunk of a near-by tree, and see what interesting neighbors you will soon have. One summer I brought home from one of my walks to the woods a section, two or three feet long, of a large yellow birch limb which contained such a cavity as I speak of, and I wired it to one of the posts of the rustic porch at Woodchuck Lodge. The next season a pair of bluebirds reared two broods in it. The incubation of the eggs for the second brood was well under way when I appeared upon the scene in early July. My sudden presence so near their treasures, and my lingering there with books and newspapers, disturbed the birds a good deal. The first afternoon the mother bird did not enter the cavity for hours. I shall always remember the pretty and earnest manner in which the male tried to reassure her and persuade her that the danger was not so imminent as it appeared to be, probably encouraging a confidence in his mate which he did not himself share. The mother bird would alight at the entrance to the chamber, but, with her eye fixed upon the man with the newspaper, feared to enter. The male, perched upon the telegraph wire fifty feet away, would raise his wings and put all the love and assurance in his voice he was capable of, apparently trying to dispel her fears. He would warble and warble, and make those pretty wing gestures over and over, saying so plainly: "It is all right, my dear, the man is harmless—absorbed there in his newspaper. Go in, go in, and keep warm our precious eggs!" How long she hesitated! But as night grew near she grew more and more anxious, and he more and more eloquent. Finally she alighted upon the edge of the overhanging roof and peered down hesitatingly. Her mate applauded and encouraged till finally she made the plunge and entered the hole, but instantly came out again; her heart failed her for a moment; but she soon returned and remained inside. Then her mate flew away toward the orchard, uttering a cheery note which doubtless she understood.

The birds soon became used to my presence and their household matters progressed satisfactorily. Both birds took a hand in feeding the young, which grew rapidly. When they were nearly ready to leave the nest, a cruel fate befell them: I slept upon the porch, and one night I was awakened by the cry of young bluebirds, and the sound of feet like those of a squirrel on the roof over me. Then I heard the cry of a young bird proceed from the butternut-tree across the road opposite the house. I said to myself, "A squirrel or an owl is after my birds." The cry coming so quickly from the butternut-tree made me suspect an owl, and that the bird whose cry I heard was in his talons. I was out of my cot and up to the nest in a moment, but the tragedy was over; the birds were all gone, and the night was silent. In the morning I found that a piece of the brittle birch limb had been torn away, enlarging the entrance to the cavity so that the murderous talons of the owl could reach in and seize the young birds. I had been aroused in time to hear the marauder on the roof with one, and then hear its cry as he carried it to the tree. In the grass in front I found one of the young, unable to fly, but apparently unhurt. I put it back in the nest, but it would not stay. The spell of the nest was broken, and the young bird took to the grass again. The parent birds were on hand, much excited, and, when I tried to return the surviving bird to the nest, the male came at me fiercely, apparently charging the whole catastrophe to me.

We had strong proof the previous season that an owl, probably the screech owl, prowled about the house at night. A statuette of myself in clay which a sculptor was modeling was left out one night on the porch, and in the morning its head was unusually bowed. The prints of a bird's talons upon the top told what had happened. In the bronze reproduction of that statuette the head has more of a droop than the artist at first planned to give it.

The next season the bluebirds occupied the cavity in the birch limb again, but before my arrival in July the owls had again cleaned them out. In so doing they had ripped the cavity open nearly to the bottom. For all that, early the following May bluebirds were occupying the cavity again. It held three eggs when I arrived. I looked over the situation and resolved to try to head off the owl this time, even at the risk of driving the bluebirds away. I took a strip of tin several inches wide and covered the slit with it and wired it fast. Then I obtained a broad strip of dry birch-bark, wrapped it about the limb over the tin, and wired it fast, leaving the entrance to the nest in its original form. I knew the owl could not slit the tin; the birch-bark would hide it and preserve in a measure the natural appearance of the branch. When the bluebirds saw what had happened to their abode, they were a good deal distressed; they could no longer see their eggs through the slit which the owl had made, and they refused to enter the cavity. They hung about all day, uttering despondent notes, approaching the nest at times, but hesitating even to alight upon the roof above it. Occasionally the female would fly away toward the distant woods or hills uttering that plaintive, homesick note which seemed to mean farewell. The male would follow her, calling in a more cheery and encouraging tone. Once the couple were gone three or four hours, and I concluded they had really deserted the place. But just before sundown they were back again, and the female alighted at the entrance to the nest and looked in. The male called to her cheerily; still she would not enter, but joined him on the telephone wire, where the two seemed to hold a little discussion. Presently the mother bird flew to the nest again, then to the roof above it, then back to the nest, and entered it till only her tail showed, then flew back to the wire beside her mate. She was evidently making up her mind that the case was not hopeless. After a little more maneuvering, and amid the happy, reassuring calls of her mate, she entered the nest cavity and remained, and I was as well pleased as was her mate.

No owls disturbed them this time, and the brood of young birds was brought off in due season. In July a second brood of four was successfully reared and sent forth on their career.

The oriole nests in many kinds of trees—oaks, maples, apple-trees, elms—but her favorite is the elm. She chooses the end of one of the long drooping branches where a group of small swaying twigs affords her suitable support. It is the most unlikely place imaginable for any but a pendent nest, woven to half a dozen or more slender, vertical twigs, and swaying freely in the wind. Few nests are so secure, so hidden, and so completely sheltered from the rains by the drooping leaves above and around it. It is rarely discoverable except from directly beneath it. I think a well-built oriole's nest would sustain a weight of eight or ten pounds before it would be torn from its moorings. They are also very partial to the ends of branches that swing low over the highway. One May I saw two female orioles building their nests twenty or twenty-five feet above our State Road, where automobiles and other vehicles passed nearly every minute all the day. An oriole's nest in a remote field far from highways and dwellings is a rare occurrence.

Birds of different species differ as widely in skill in nest-building as they do in song. From the rude platform of dry twigs and other coarse material of the cuckoo, to the pendent, closely woven pouch of the oriole, the difference in the degree of skill displayed is analogous to the difference between the simple lisp of the cedar-bird, or the little tin whistle of the "chippie," and the golden notes of the wood thrush, or the hilarious song of the bobolink.

Real castles in the air are the nests of the orioles; no other nests are better hidden or apparently more safe from the depredations of crows and squirrels. To start the oriole's nest successfully is quite an engineering feat. The birds inspect the branches many times before they make a decision. When they have decided on the site, the mother bird brings her first string or vegetable fiber and attaches it to a twig by winding it around and around many times, leaving one or both ends hanging free. I have nests where these foundation strings are wound around a twig a dozen times. In her blind windings and tuckings and loopings the bird occasionally ties a substantial knot, but it is never the result of a deliberate purpose as some observers contend, but purely a matter of chance. When she uses only wild vegetable fibers, she fastens it to the twig by a hopeless kind of tangle. It is about the craziest kind of knitting imaginable. After the builder has fastened many lines to opposite twigs, their ends hanging free, she proceeds to span the little gulf by weaving them together. She stands with her claws clasped one to each side, and uses her beak industriously, looping up and fastening the loose ends. I have stood in the road under the nest looking straight up till my head swam, trying to make out just how she did it, but all I could see was the bird standing astride the chasm she was trying to bridge, and busy with the hanging strings. Slowly the maze of loose threads takes a sacklike form, the bottom of the nest thickens, till some morning you see the movement of the bird inside it; her beak comes through the sides from within, like a needle or an awl, seizes a loose hair or thread, and jerks it back through the wall and tightens it. It is a regular stitching or quilting process. The course of any particular thread or fiber is as irregular and haphazard as if it were the work of the wind or the waves. There is plan, but no conscious method of procedure. In fact, a bird's nest is a growth. It is not something builded as we build, in which judgment, design, forethought enter; it is the result of the blind groping of instinct which rarely errs, but which does not see the end from the beginning, as reason does. The oriole sometimes overhands the rim of her nest with strings and fibers to make it firm, and to afford a foundation for her to perch upon, but it is like the pathetic work which an untaught blind child might do under similar conditions. The birds use fine, strong strings in their nest-building at their peril. Many a tragedy results from it. I have an oriole's nest sent me from Michigan on the outside of which is a bird's dried foot with a string ingeniously knotted around it. It would be difficult to tie so complicated a knot. The tragedy is easy to read. Another nest sent me from the Mississippi Valley is largely made up of fragments of fish-line with the fish-hooks on them. But there is no sign that the bird came to grief using this dangerous material. Where the lives of the wild creatures impinge upon our lives is always a danger-line to them. They are partakers of our bounty in many ways, but they pay a tax to fate in others.

The orioles in my part of the country always use the same material in the body of their nests—a kind of soft, gray, flaxlike fiber which they apparently get from some species of everlasting flower. Woven together and quilted through with strings and horse-hairs, it makes strong, warm, feltlike walls. In the nest sent me from Michigan the walls are made of something that suggests brown human hair, except that it is too hard and brittle for hair.

Our orchard oriole also makes a pendent nest, but not so deep and pocketlike as that of the Baltimore oriole, and showing no such elaborate use of strings and hairs. It is made entirely of some sort of dried grass, very elaborately woven together.

Bullock's oriole of California weaves its nest entirely of the long, strong threads which it draws out of the palm-leaves. The only one I have seen was suspended from the under side of one of those leaves.

I think the prize nest of the woods, if we except the nest of the hummingbird, is that of the wood pewee. It is as smooth and compact and symmetrical as if turned in a lathe out of some soft, feltlike substance. Of course, the ph[oe]be's artistic masonry under the shelving rocks, covered with moss and lined with feathers, or with the finest dry grass and bark fibers, sheltered from the storms and beyond the reach of four-footed prowlers, is almost ideal. It certainly is a happy thought.

The least flycatcher, the kingbird, the cedar-bird, the goldfinch, the indigo-bird, are all fine nest-builders, each with a style of its own.

About the most insecure nest in our trees is that of the little social sparrow, or "chippie." When the sudden summer storms come, making the tree-tops writhe as if in agony, I think of this frail nest amid the tossing branches. Pass through the grove or orchard after the tempest is over, and you are pretty sure to find several wrecked nests upon the ground. "Chippie" has never learned the art of nest-building in trees. She is a poor architect. She should have kept to the ground or to the low bushes. The true tree nest-builders weave their nests fast to the branches, but "Chippie" does not; she simply arranges her material loosely between them, where the nest is supported, but not secured. She seems pathetically ignorant of the fact that there are such things as wind and storm. Hence her frail structure is more frequently dislodged from the trees than that of any other bird.

Recently, after a day of violent northwest wind, I found a wrecked robin's nest and eggs upon the lawn under a maple—not a frequent spectacle. The robin's firm masonry is usually proof against wind and rain, but in this case the nest was composed almost entirely of dry grass; there was hardly a trace of mud in it, hence it was flexible and yielding, and had no grip of the branches. It was evidently the second nest of the pair this season, and the second nest in summer of any species of bird is frailer and more of a makeshift than the first nest in spring. Comparatively few of our birds attempt to bring off a second brood unless the first attempt has been defeated, but the robin is sure to bring off two, and may bring off three. But the robin is a hustler, probably the most enterprising of all our birds. I recall a mother robin that, in late June, repaired a nest in a climbing rosebush which her first brood had vacated only a week before. A brood of wood thrushes which left their nest about the same time was still being fed by their parents about the place.

The song sparrow, the social sparrow, the ph[oe]be, the bluebird, all build a second nest. The first brood of the bluebird will be looked after by the father in some near-by grove or orchard, while the mother starts a new family in the old nest. If all goes well with them, those two bluebird families will unite and keep together in a loose flock till they migrate in the fall.

So many of our birds nest about our houses and lawns and gardens and along our highways, that at first sight it seems as if they must be drawn there by a sense of greater security for their eggs and young. The robin has become almost a domestic institution. It is rarely that one finds a robin's nest very far from a human habitation. One spring there were four robins' nests on my house and outbuildings—in the vines, on window-sills, or other coigns of vantage. There were at the same time at least fifteen robins' nests on my lot of sixteen acres, and I am quite certain that I have not seen all there were. They were in sheds and apple-trees and spruces and cedars, in the ends of piles of grape-posts, in rosebushes, in the summer-house, and on the porch. We did not expect to get one of the early cherries, and might count ourselves lucky if we got any of the later ones.

A robin has built her nest in my summer-house. She abuses me so when I try to tarry there, after incubation has begun, that I take no comfort and presently withdraw. Until her brood has flown, I am practically a stranger in my open-air rest-house and study.

When the fish crows come egging in the spruces and maples about the house, and I hear the screaming of the robins, I seize my gun and rush out to protect them, but am not always successful, as the mischief is often done before I get within reach; I am not sure but that the robins think—if they think at all—that

I am in league with the crows to despoil them. I was not in time to save the eggs of the wood thrush the other morning, when I heard the alarm calls of the birds, but I had the satisfaction of seeing the black marauder go limping over the hill, dropping quills from his wings at nearly every stroke. I am sure he will not come back. The fish crow is one of the most active enemies of our small birds. Of course, he only obeys his instincts in hunting out and devouring their eggs and young, but I fancy I obey something higher than instinct when I protest with powder and shot.

The birds do not mind the approach of the domestic animals, such as the cow, the horse, the sheep, the pig, and they are only a little suspicious of the dog, but the appearance of the cat fills them with sudden alarm. I think that birds that have never before seen a cat join in the hue and cry. What alarms one alarms all within hearing. The orioles are probably the most immune from the depredations of crows and jays and owls of all our birds, and yet they will join in the cry of "Thief, thief!" when a crow appears. (The alarm cry of birds will even arrest the attention of four-footed beasts, and often bring the sportsman's stalking to naught.)

I fancy that Ph[oe]be selects our sheds and bridges and porticoes for her nesting-sites because they are so much more numerous than the overhanging rocks where her forbears built. For the same reason certain of the swallows and the swifts select our barns and chimneys.

If the birds themselves are not afraid to draw near us, why should their instinct lead them to feel that their enemies will be afraid of us? How do they know that a jay or a crow or a red squirrel will be less timid than they are? And why also, if they have such confidence in us, do they raise such a hue and cry when we pass near their nests? The robin in my summer-house knew, if she knew anything, that I had never raised a finger against her. On the contrary, my hoe in the garden had unearthed many a worm and slug for her. Still she sees in me only a possible enemy, and tolerate me with my book or my newspaper near her nest she will not. Another robin has built her nest in a rosebush that has been trained to form an arch over the walk that leads to the kitchen door and only a few yards from it; but whenever we pass and repass she scurries away with loud, angry protests and keeps it up as long as we are in sight, so that we do not feel at all complimented by her settling down so near us. If one's appearance is so alarming, even when he is going to hoe the garden, why did the intolerant bird set up her household gods so near? If I keep away her enemies, why will she not be gracious enough to regard me as her friend? The robin that trusted her brood to the sheltering vines of the woodshed, and lined her nest with the hair of our old gray horse—why should she scream, "Murder!" whenever any of us go to the well a few feet away?

What is the real explanation of the fact that so many of our birds nest so near our dwellings and yet show such unfriendliness when we come near them? Their apparent confidence, on the one hand, contradicts their suspicion on the other. Is it because we have here the workings of a new instinct which has not yet adjusted itself to the workings of the older instinct of solicitude for the safety of the nest and young? My own interpretation is that birds are not drawn near us by any sense of greater security in our vicinity. It is evident from the start that there is an initial fear of us to be overcome. How, then, could the sense of greater safety in our presence arise? Fear and trust do not spring from the same root. How should the robins and thrushes know that their enemies—the jays, the crows, and the like—are more afraid of human beings than they are themselves? Hunted animals pursued by wolves or hounds will at times take refuge in the haunts of men, not because they expect human protection, but because they are desperate, and oblivious to everything save some means of escape. If the hunted deer or fox rushes into an open shed or a barn door, it is because it is desperately hard-pressed, and sees and knows nothing but some object or situation that it may place between itself and its deadly enemy. The great fear obliterates all minor fears.

The key to the behavior of the birds in this respect may be found in the Darwinian theory of natural selection. From the first settlement of the country a few of the common birds, attracted by a more suitable or more abundant food-supply, or other conditions, must inevitably have nested near human dwellings. These birds would thrive better and succeed in bringing off more young than those that nested in more exposed places. Hence, their progeny would soon be in the ascendancy. All animals seem to have associated memory. These birds would naturally return to the scenes and conditions of their youth, and start their nests there. It would not be confidence in men that would draw them; rather would the truth be that the fear of man is inadequate to overcome or annul this home attraction.

The catbird does not come to our vines on the veranda to nest from considerations of safety, but because her line of descent runs through such places. The catbirds and robins and ph[oe]be-birds that were reared far from human habitations doubtless return to such localities to rear their young. The home sense in birds is strong. I have positive proof in a few instances of robins and song sparrows returning successive years to the same neighborhood. It is very certain, I think, that the ph[oe]be-birds that daub our porches with their mud, and in July leave a trail of minute creeping and crawling pests, were not themselves hatched and reared in the pretty, moss-covered structure under the shelving rocks in the woods, or on the hillsides.

How different from the manners of the robins are the manners of a pair of catbirds that have a nest in the honeysuckle against the side of the first-floor sleeping-porch! Nothing seems farther from the nature of the catbird than the hue and cry which the robin at times sets up. The catbird is sly and dislikes publicity. An appealing feline *mew* is her characteristic note. She never raises her voice like the town-crier, as the robin does, perched in the mean time where all eyes may behold him. The catbird peers and utters her soft protest from her hiding-place in the bushes. This particular pair of catbirds appeared in early May and began slyly to look over the situation in the vines and bushes about the house. All their proceedings were very stealthy; they were like two dark shadows gliding about, avoiding observation—no tree-tops or house-tops for them, but coverts close to the ground. We hoped they would divine safety in the shadow of the cottage, but tried to act as if oblivious of their goings and comings. We saw them now and then stealthily inspecting the tangle of honeysuckle on the east side of the veranda, where a robin last season reared a brood, and the low hedge of barberry-bushes on the south side of the cottage, where a song sparrow had her nest. If they come, which will they take, we wondered. Several times in the early morning I heard the male singing vivaciously and confidently in the thick of the honeysuckle. I guessed that the honeysuckle was the choice of the male, and that his song was a pæan in praise of it, addressed to his mate. But it was nearly a week before his musical argument prevailed and the site was apparently agreed upon.

When the nest-building actually began, the birds were so shy about it that, watch as I might, I failed to catch them in the act. One morning I saw the mother bird in the garden with nesting-material in her beak, but she failed to come to the honeysuckle with it while I watched from a near-by covert. At the same time robins were flying here and there with loaded beaks, and wood thrushes were going through the air trailing long strips of white paper behind them, but the catbird was an emblem of secrecy itself. She, too, brought fragments of white paper to her nest, but no one saw her do it. Like other nest-builders, she apparently put in her big strokes of work in the early morning before the sleepers on the veranda were stirring. A few times my inquisitive eye, cautiously peering over the railing, started her from the vine, but I never saw her enter it with leaf, stick, or straw; yet slowly the nest grew and came into shape, and finally received its finishing touches. So cautiously had the birds proceeded that, were they capable of concepts like us, I should fancy they flattered themselves that we had not the least suspicion of their little secret. The male ceased to sing near the house after the nest was begun. So much time elapsed after the finishing of the nest before the first egg appeared in it that some members of the household feared the birds had deserted it, especially as they were not seen about the premises for several days. But the weather was wet and cool, and the eggs ripened slowly. Then one morning the birds were seen again, and one blue-green egg was discovered in the nest. The next morning another egg was added, and a third egg on the third morning, and a fourth on the fourth morning. In due time incubation began, and thenceforth all went well with our dusky neighbors.

It is an anxious moment for all birds when their young leave the nest. One noontime by the unusual mewing of a parent catbird I felt sure that the critical time had come. Sure enough, there sat one of the young on a twig a few inches above the nest, motionless and hushed. No lusty response to the agitated cry of the mother, as is usually the case with the robin. "No publicity" is the watchword of the young catbirds as well as of the old. An hour or two later another young one was perched on a branch, and before night, when no one was looking, they both disappeared, leaving two motionless birds in the nest. The next morning early, without any signs of alarm or agitation on the part of the old birds, they took the important step. It could hardly have been much of a flight with any of them, as their wing-quills were only partially developed, and their tails were mere stubs. For several days afterward no sign or sound of old or young was seen or heard. They were probably keeping well concealed in the near-by trees or in the vines and currant-bushes in the vineyard. In about a week the whole family appeared briefly in upper branches of the maples near the house. The young were distinguishable from the old only by their shorter tails. A few days later the parent birds were seen moving stealthily through the vines and bushes about the house, or perching on the near-by stakes that supported the wire netting. Are they coming back for a second brood? was the question in our minds.

Soon we began to hear snatches of song from the male, then one morning a regular old-time burst of joy from him in the vine that held the old nest. Then he sang in a syringa-bush near the window on the south side of the cottage, and both birds were soon seen paying frequent visits to the bush. We felt sure another brood was in the air. Whether or not the first brood were now shifting for themselves, we did not know; they never again appeared upon the scene. Finally, on the morning of the Fourth of July, the foundation of a new nest was started in the syringa-bush three feet from the ground, and barely four feet from the window!

We had a view of the proceedings that the first site did not afford us. The old nest appeared to be in perfect condition, but there was evidently no thought with the birds of using it again, as the robins sometimes do, and as bluebirds and cliff swallows always do. A new nest, built of material almost identical with that of the old, and in a more exposed position, was decided upon. It progressed rapidly, and I was delighted to find that the male assisted in the building. Indeed, he was fully as active as the female. Very often they were both in the nest with material at the same moment. They seemed to agree perfectly. At first I got the impression that the male was not quite as decided as the female, and hesitated more, once or twice bringing material that he finally rejected. But he soon warmed up to the work and certainly did his share.

With most species of our birds the nest is entirely built by the female. With the robin, the wood thrush, the ph[oe]be, the oriole, the hummingbird, the pewee, and many others, the male is only an interested spectator of the proceeding. He usually attends his mate in her quest for material, but does not lend a hand, or a bill. I think the cock wren assists in nest-building. I know the male cedar-bird does, and probably the male woodpeckers do also. The male rose-breasted grosbeak assists in incubation, and has been seen to sing upon the nest. It seems fair to infer that he assists in the nest-building also, but I am not certain that he does, and I have heard another observer state that in a nest which he watched the female apparently did it all.

My catbirds both worked overtime one afternoon at least, being on their job as late as seven o'clock. In three days the nest was done, all but touching up the interior. During the construction I laid out pieces of twine and bits of white paper on the bushes and wire netting, also some loose material from the outside of the old nest; all was quickly used. How much labor the birds would have saved themselves had they pulled the old nest to pieces and used the material a second time! I have known the oriole to start a nest, then change her mind, and then detach some of her strings and fibers and carry them to the new site; and I once saw a "chebec" whose eggs had been destroyed pull the old nest to pieces and rebuild it in a tree a hundred feet away.

The male catbird is slightly brighter and fresher-looking than his mate, but we could easily tell her by her often simulating the actions of a young bird when she came with material in her beak; she would alight on a near-by post and slightly spread and quiver her wings in a tender, beseeching kind of way. She would do this also when bringing food to her first brood. When one of the parent birds of any species simulates by voice or manner the young birds, it is always the female; her heart would naturally be more a-quiver with anticipation than that of the male.

On the fifth day the nest was completed and received its first egg. There was considerable delay with the second egg, but it appeared on the second or third day, and the third egg the following day. Then incubation began. In twenty days from the day the nest was begun, the birds were hatched, and in eleven days more they had quietly left the nest.

A friend of mine who has a summer home on one of the trout-streams of the Catskills discovered that the catbird was fond of butter, and she soon had one of the birds coming every day to the dining-room window for its lump of fresh butter, and finally entering the dining-room, perching on the back of the chair, and receiving its morsel of butter from a fork held in the mistress's hand. I think the butter was unsalted. My friend was convinced after three years that the same pair of birds returned to her each year, because each season the male came promptly for his butter.

The furtive and stealthy manners of the catbird contrast strongly with the frank, open manners of the thrushes. Its cousin the brown thrasher goes skulking about in much the same way, flirting from bush to bush like a culprit escaping from justice. But he does love to sing from the April tree-tops where all the world may see and hear, if said world does not come too near. In the South and West the thrasher also nests in the vicinity of houses, but in New York and New England we must look for him in remote, bushy fields. I do not know of any bad traits that go with the thrasher's air of suspicion and secrecy, but I do know of one that goes with the catbird's—I have seen her perch on the rim of another bird's nest and deliberately devour the eggs. But only once. Whether or not she frequently does this, I have no evidence. If she does, she is doubtless so sly about it that she escapes observation.

I welcomed the catbird, though she is not so attractive a neighbor as the wood thrush. She has none of the wood thrush's dignity and grace. She skulks and slinks away like a culprit, while the wood thrush stands up before you or perches upon a limb, and turns his spotted waistcoat toward you in the most open and trusting manner. In fact, few birds have such good manners as the wood thrush, and few have so much the manner of a Paul Pry and eavesdropper as the catbird. The flight of the wood thrush across the lawn is such a picture of grace and harmony, it is music to the eye. The catbird seems saying, "There, there! I told you so, pretty figure, pretty figure you make!" But the courteous thrush (just here I heard the excited calls of robins and the hoarse, angry caw of a crow, and rushed out hatless to see a fish crow fly away from the maple in front of the Study, pursued by a mob of screeching robins. He took refuge in the spruces above the house where the collected robins abused him from surrounding branches. On my appearance he flew away, and the robins dispersed)—but the courteous thrush, I say, invites the good-breeding in you which he himself shows. The thrush never has the air of a culprit, while the catbird seldom has any other air. But I welcome them both. One shall stand for the harmony and repose of bird life, and the other for its restlessness and curiosity. The songs and the manners of birds correspond. The catbird, the brown thrasher, and the mockingbird are all theatrical in their manners—full of gestures of tail and wings, and their songs all imply an audience, while the serene melody of the thrushes is in keeping with the grace and poise of their behavior.

V

A MIDSUMMER IDYL

As I sit here of a midsummer day, in front of the wide-open doors of a big hay-barn, busy with my pen, and look out upon broad meadows where my farmer neighbor is busy with his haymaking, I idly contrast his harvest with mine. I have to admit that he succeeds with his better than I do with mine, though he can make hay only while the sun shines, while I can reap and cure my light fancies nearly as well in the shade as in the sun. Yet his crop is the surer and of more certain value to mankind. But I have this advantage over him—I might make literature out of his haymaking, or might reap his fields after him, and gather a harvest he never dreamed of. What does Emerson say?

> One harvest from the field
>   Homeward bring the oxen strong;
> A second crop thine acres yield,
>   Which I gather in a song.

But the poet, like the farmer, can reap only where he has sown, and if Emerson had not scattered his own heart in the fields his Muse would not reap much there. Song is not one of the instruments with which I gather my harvest, but long ago, as a farm boy, in haymaking, and in driving the cows to and from the pasture, I planted myself there, and whatever comes back to me now from that source is honestly my own. The second crop which I gather is not much more tangible than that which the poet gathers, but the farmer as little suspects its existence as he does that of the poet. I can use what he would gladly reject. His daisies, his buttercups, his orange hawkweed, his yarrow, his meadow-rue, serve my purpose better than they do his. They look better on the printed page than they do in the haymow. Yes, and his timothy and clover have their literary uses, and his new-mown hay may perfume a line in poetry. When one of our poets writes, "wild carrot blooms nod round his quiet bed," he makes better use of this weed than the farmers can.

Certainly a midsummer day in the country, with all its sights and sounds, its singing birds, its skimming swallows, its grazing or ruminating cattle, its drifting cloud-shadows, its grassy perfumes from the meadows and the hillsides, and the farmer with his men and teams busy with the harvest, has material for the literary artist. A good hay day is a good day for the writer and the poet, because it has a certain crispness and pureness; it is positive; it is rich in sunshine; there is a potency in the blue sky which you feel; the high barometer raises your spirits; your thoughts ripen as the hay cures. You can sit in a circle of shade beneath a tree in the fields, or in front of the open hay-barn doors, as I do, and feel the fruition and satisfaction of nature all about you. The brimming meadows seem fairly to purr as the breezes stroke them; the trees rustle their myriad leaves as if in gladness; the many-colored butterflies dance by; the steel blue of the swallows' backs glistens in the sun as they skim the fields; and the mellow boom of the passing bumble-bee but enhances the sense of repose and contentment that pervades the air. The hay cures; the oats and corn deepen their hue; the delicious fragrance of the last wild strawberries is on the breeze; your mental skies are lucid, and life has the midsummer fullness and charm.

As I linger here I note the oft-repeated song of the scarlet tanager in the maple woods that crown a hill above me, and in the loft overhead two broods of swallows are chattering and lining up their light-colored breasts on the rims of their nests, or trying their newly fledged wings while clinging to its sides. The only ominous and unwelcome sound is the call of the cuckoo, which I hear and have heard at nearly all hours for many days, and which surely bodes rain. The countryman who first named this bird the "rain crow" hit the mark. The cuckoo is a devourer of worms and caterpillars, and why he should be interested in rain is hard to see. The tree-toad calls before and during a shower, mainly, I think, because he likes to have his back wet, but why a well-dressed bird like the cuckoo should become a prophet of the rain is a mystery, unless the rain and the shadows are congenial to the gloomy mood in which he usually seems to be. He is the least sprightly and cheery of our birds, and the part of doleful prophet in our bird drama suits him well.

A high barometer is best for the haymakers and it is best for the human spirits. When the smoke goes straight up, one's thoughts are more likely to soar also, and revel in the higher air. The persons who do not like to get up in the morning till the day has been well sunned and aired evidently thrive best on a high barometer. Such days do seem better ventilated, and our lungs take in fuller draughts of air. How curious it is that the air should seem heavy to us when it is light, and light when it is heavy! On those sultry, muggy days when it is an effort to move, and the grasshopper is a burden, the air is light, and we are in the trough of the vast atmospheric wave; while we are on its crest, and are buoyed up both in mind and in body, on the crisp, bright days when the air seems to offer us no resistance. We know that the heavier salt sea-water buoys us up more than the fresh river or pond water, but we do not feel in the same way the lift of the high barometric wave. Even the rough, tough-coated maple-trees in spring are quickly susceptible to these atmospheric changes. The farmer knows that he needs sunshine and crisp air to make maple-sugar as well as to make hay. Let the high blue-domed day with its dry northwest breezes change to a warmer, overcast, humid day from the south, and the flow of sap lessens at once. It would seem as if the trees had nerves on the outside of their dry bark, they respond to the change so quickly. There is no sap without warmth, and yet warmth, without any memory of the frost, stops the flow.

The more the air presses upon us the lighter we feel, and the less it presses upon us the more "logy" we feel. Climb to the top of a mountain ten thousand feet high, and you breathe and move with an effort. The air is light, water boils at a low temperature, and our lungs and muscles seem inadequate to perform their usual functions. There is a kind of pressure that exhilarates us, and an absence of pressure that depresses us.

The pressure of congenial tasks, of worthy work, sets one up, while the idle, the unemployed, has a deficiency of hæmoglobin in his blood. The Lord pity the unemployed man, and pity the man so over-employed that the pressure upon him is like that upon one who works in a tunnel filled with compressed air.

Haying in this pastoral region is the first act in the drama of the harvest, and one likes to see it well staged, as it is to-day—the high blue dome, the rank, dark foliage of the trees, the daisies still white in the sun, the buttercups gilding the pastures and hill-slopes, the clover shedding its perfume, the timothy shaking out its little clouds of pollen as the sickle-bar strikes it, most of the song-birds still vocal, and the tide of summer standing poised at its full. Very soon it will begin to ebb, the stalks of the meadow grasses will become dry and harsh, the clover will fade, the girlish daisies will become coarse and matronly, the birds will sing fitfully or cease altogether, the pastures will turn brown, and the haymakers will find the hay half cured as it stands waiting for them in the meadows.

What a wonderful thing is the grass, so common, so abundant, so various, a green summer snow that softens the outlines of the landscape, that makes a carpet for the foot, that brings a hush to the fields, and that furnishes food to so many and such various creatures! More than the grazing animals live upon the grass. All our cereals—wheat, barley, rye, rice, oats, corn—belong to the great family of the grasses.

Grass is the nap of the fields; it is the undergarment of the hills. It gives us the meadow, a feature in the northern landscape so common that we cease to remark it, but which we miss at once when we enter a tropical or semi-tropical country. In Cuba and Jamaica and Hawaii I saw no meadows and no pastures, no grazing cattle, none of the genial, mellow look which our landscape presents. Harshness, rawness, aridity, are the prevailing notes.

From my barn-door outlook I behold meadows with their boundary line of stone fences that are like lakes and reservoirs of timothy and clover. They are full to the brim, they ripple and rock in the breeze, the green inundation seems about to overwhelm its boundaries, all the surface inequalities of the land are wiped out, the small rocks and stones are hidden, the woodchucks make their roads through it, immersed like dolphins in the sea. What a picture of the plenty and the flowing beneficence of our temperate zone it all presents! Nature in her kinder, gentler moods, dreaming of the tranquil herds and the bursting barns. Surely the vast army of the grass hath its victories, for the most part noiseless, peace-yielding victories that gladden the eye and tranquillize the heart.

The meadow presents a pleasing picture before it is invaded by the haymakers, and a varied and animated one after it is thus invaded; the mowing-machine sending a shudder ahead of it through the grass, the hay-tedder kicking up the green locks like a giant, many-legged grasshopper, the horserake gathering the cured hay into windrows, the white-sleeved men with their forks pitching it into cocks, and, lastly, the huge, soft-cheeked loads of hay, towering above the teams that draw them, brushing against the bar-ways and the lower branches of the trees along their course, slowly winding their way toward the barn. Then the great mows of hay, or the shapely stacks in the fields, and the battle is won. Milk and cream are stored up in well-cured hay, and when the snow of winter fills the meadows as grass fills them in summer, the tranquil cow can still rest and ruminate in contentment.

As the swallows sweep out and in near my head they give out an angry "Sleet, sleet," as if my presence had suddenly become offensive to them. I know what makes the change in their temper. The young are leaving their nests, and at such eventful times the parent birds are always nervous and anxious. When any of our birds launch a family into the world they would rather not have spectators, and you are pretty sure to be abused if you intrude upon the scene. The swallow can put a good deal of sharp emphasis into that "Sleet, sleet," though she is not armed to make any of her threats good. Who knows that all will go well with them when they first make the plunge into space with their untried wings? A careful parent should keep the coast clear.

They have been testing their wings for several days, clinging to the sides of the nest and beating the wings rapidly. And now comes the crucial moment of letting go and attempting actual flight. Several of them have already done it, and I see them resting on the dead limbs of a plum-tree across the road. But more are to follow, and parental anxiety is still rife. I shall be sorry when the spacious hayloft becomes silent. That affectionate "Wit, wit" and that contented and caressing squeaking and chattering give me a sense of winged companionship. The old barn is the abode of friendly and delicate spirits, and the sight of them and the sound of them surely bring a suggestion of poetry and romance to these familiar scenes.

Is not the swallow one of the oldest and dearest of birds? Known to the poets and sages and prophets of all peoples! So infantile, so helpless and awkward upon the earth, so graceful and masterful on the wing, the child and darling of the summer air, reaping its invisible harvest in the fields of space as if it dined on the sunbeams, touching no earthly food, drinking and bathing and mating on the wing, swiftly, tirelessly coursing the long day through, a thought on wings, a lyric in the shape of a bird! Only in the free fields of the summer air could it have got that steel-blue of the wings and that warm tan of the breast. Of course I refer to the barn swallow. The cliff swallow seems less a child of the sky and sun, probably because its sheen and glow are less, and its shape and motions less arrowy. More varied in color, its hues yet lack the intensity, and its flight the swiftness, of those of its brother of the haylofts. The tree swallows and the bank swallows are pleasing, but they are much more local and restricted in their ranges than the barn-frequenters. As a farm boy I did not know them at all, but the barn swallows the summer always brought.

After all, there is but one swallow; the others are particular kinds that we specify. How curious that men should ever have got the notion that this airy, fairy creature, this playmate of the sunbeams, spends the winter hibernating in the mud of ponds and marshes, the bedfellow of newts and frogs and turtles! It is an Old-World legend, born of the blindness and superstition of earlier times. One knows that the rain of the rainbow may be gathered at one's feet in a mud-puddle, but the fleeting spectrum of the bow is not a thing of life. Yet one would as soon think of digging up a rainbow in the mud as a swallow. The swallow follows the sun, and in August is off for the equatorial regions, where it hibernates on the wing, buried in tropical sunshine.

Well, this brilliant day is a good day for the swallows, a good day for the haymakers, and a good day for him who sits before his open barn door and weaves his facts and midsummer fancies into this slight literary fabric.

VI

NEAR VIEWS OF WILD LIFE

The wild life around us is usually so unobtrusive and goes its own way so quietly and furtively that we miss much of it unless we cultivate an interest in it. A person must be interested in it, to paraphrase a line of Wordsworth's, ere to him it will seem worthy of his interest. One thing is linked to another or gives a clue to another. There is no surer way to find birds' nests than to go berrying or fishing. In the blackberry or raspberry bushes you may find the bush sparrow's nest or the indigobird's nest. Once while fishing a trout-stream I missed my fish, and my hook caught on a branch over my head. When I pulled the branch down, there, deftly saddled upon it, was a hummingbird's nest. I unwittingly caught more than I missed. On another occasion I stumbled upon the nest of the water accentor which I had never before found; on still another, upon the nest of the winter wren, a marvel of mossy softness and delicacy hidden under a mossy log.

Along trout-streams with overhanging or shelving ledges the fisherman often sees the nest of the ph[oe]be-bird, which does not cease to please for the hundredth time, because of its fitness and exquisite artistry. On the newly sawn timbers of your porch or woodshed it is far less pleasing, because the bird's art, born of rocky ledges, only serves in the new environment to make its nest conspicuous.

Sitting in my barn-door study I see a vesper sparrow fly up and alight on the telephone wire with nesting-material in her beak. I keep my eye upon her. In a moment she drops down to the grassy and weedy bank of the roadside in front of me and disappears. A few moments later I have her secret—a nest in a little recess in the bank. That straw gave the finishing touch. She kept her place on the nest until she had deposited her first egg on June 24th, probably for her second brood this season. Some young vespers flitting about farther up the road are presumably her first brood. Each day thereafter for four consecutive days she added an egg. Incubation soon began and on the 10th of July the young were out, the little sprawling, skinny things looking, as a city girl said when she first beheld newly-hatched birds in a nest, as if they were mildewed.

These ground-builders among the birds, taking their chances in the great common of the open fields, at the mercy of all their enemies every hour—the hoofs of grazing cattle, prowling skunks, foxes, weasels, coons by night, and crows and hawks by day—what bird-lover does not experience a little thrill when in his walk he comes upon one of their nests? He has found a thing of art among the unkempt and the disorderly; he has found a thing of life and love amid the cold and the insensate. Yet all so artless and natural! Every shred and straw of it serves a purpose; it fairly warms and vivifies the little niche in which it is placed. What a center of solicitude and forethought.

Not many yards below the vesper's nest, on the other side of the road, is a junco's nest. You may know the junco's nest from that of any other ground-builder by its being more elaborate and more perfectly hidden. The nest is tucked far under the mossy and weedy bank, and only a nest-hunter passing along the road, with "eye practiced like a blind man's touch" and with juncos in mind, would have seen it. A little screen of leaves of the hawkweed permits only the rim of one edge of the nest to be seen. Not till I stooped down and reached forth my hand did the mother bird come fluttering out and go down the road with drooping wings and spread tail, the white quills of the latter fairly lighting up the whole performance.

A very shy and artful bird is the junco. I had had brief glimpses of the male many times about the place. The morning I found the nest I had seen one male spitefully pursuing another male along the top of the stone wall opposite, which fact, paralleled in a human case, would afford a hint for detectives to work on. The junco is evidently a very successful bird. The swarms of them that one sees in the late fall and in the early winter going south is good evidence of this. They usually precede the white-throats north in the spring, but a few linger and breed in the high altitude of the Catskills.

When the sun shines hot the sparrow in front of my door makes herself into a sunshade to protect her nestlings. She pants with the heat, and her young pant too; they would probably perish were not the direct rays of the sun kept from them. Another vesper sparrow's nest yonder in the hill pasture, from which we flushed the bird in our walk, might be considered in danger from a large herd of dairy cows, but it is wisely placed in view of such a contingency. It is at the foot of a stalk of Canada thistle about a foot and a half high, and where, for a few square yards, the grazing is very poor. I do not think that the chances are one in fifty that the hoof of a cow will find it. I do not suppose that the problem presented itself to the bird as it does to me, but her instinct was as sure a guide as my reason is to me—or a surer one.

The vesper sparrow was thus happily named by a New England bird-lover, Wilson Flagg, an old-fashioned writer on our birds, fifty or more years ago. I believe the bird was called the grass finch by our earlier writers. It haunts the hilly pastures and roadsides in the Catskill region. It is often called the road-runner, from its habit of running along the road ahead when one is driving or walking—a very different bird, however, from the road-runner of the Western States. The vesper is larger than the song sparrow, of a lighter gray and russet, and does not frequent our gardens and orchards as does the latter. In color it suggests the European skylark; the two lateral white quills in its tail enhance this impression. One season a stray skylark, probably from Long Island or some other place where larks had been liberated, appeared in a broad, low meadow near me, and not finding his own kind paid court to a female vesper sparrow. He pursued her diligently and no doubt pestered her dreadfully. She fled from him precipitately and seemed much embarrassed by the attentions of the distinguished-looking foreigner.

When the young of any species appear, the solicitude and watchfulness of the mother bird are greatly increased. Although my near neighbor the vesper sparrow in front of my door has had proof of my harmless character now for several weeks and, one would think, must know that her precious secret is safe with me, yet, when she comes with food in her beak while I am at my desk ten or eleven yards away, she maneuvers around for a minute or two, flying up to the telephone wire or a few yards up or down the road, and finally approaches the nest with much hesitation and suspicion, lest I see her in the act. When she comes again and again and again, she is filled with the same apprehension.

After a night of heavy but warm rain two of the half-fledged young were lying on the ground in front of the nest, dead. There were no murderous marks upon them, and the secret of the tragedy I could not divine.

What automatons these wild creatures are, apparently so wise on some occasions and so absurd on others! This vesper sparrow in bringing food to her young, going through the same tactics over and over, learns no more than a machine would. But, of course, the bird does not think; hence the folly of her behavior to a being that does. The wisdom of nature, which is so unerring under certain conditions, becomes to us sheer folly under changed conditions.

When the mother bird's suspicion gets the better of her, she often devours the food she has in her beak, so fearful is she of betraying her precious secret. But the next time she comes she may only maneuver briefly before approaching the nest, and then again hesitate and parley with her fears and make false moves and keep her eye on me, as if I had only just appeared upon the scene.

One of the best things a bird-lover can have in front of his house or cabin is a small dead tree with numerous leafless branches. Many kinds of birds love to perch briefly where they can look around them. I would not exchange the old dead plum-tree that stands across the road in front of my lodge for the finest living plum-tree in the world. It bears a perpetual crop of birds. Of course the strictly sylvan birds, such as the warblers, the vireos, the oven-bird, the veery and hermit thrushes, do not come, but many kinds of other birds pause there during the day and seem to enjoy the unobstructed view.

All the field and orchard and grove birds come. In early summer the bobolink perches there, then tiptoes, or tip-wings, away to the meadows below,pouring out his ecstatic song. The rose-breasted grosbeak comes and shows his brilliant front. The purple finch, the goldfinch, the indigo bunting, the bluebird, the kingbird, the ph[oe]be-bird, the great crested flycatcher, the robin, the oriole, the chickadee, the high-hole, the downy woodpecker, the vesper sparrow, the social sparrow, or chippy, pause there in the course of the day, and some of them several times during the day. Occasionally the scarlet tanager lights it up with his vivid color.

But more than all it is the favorite perch of a song sparrow whose mate has a nest not far off. Here he perches and goes through his repertoire of three or four different songs from dawn till nightfall, pausing only long enough now and then to visit his mate or to refresh himself with a little food. He repeats his strain six times a minute, often preening his plumage in the intervals. He sings several hundred times a day and has been doing so for many weeks. The house wren during the breeding-season repeats his song thousands of times a day, while the red-eyed vireo sings continuously from morning till night for several months. How a conscious effort like that would weary our human singers and their hearers! But the birds are quite unconscious, in our sense, of what they are doing.

When we pause to think of it, what a spectacle this singing sparrow presents! A little wild bird sitting on a dead branch and lifting up its voice in song hour after hour, day after day, week after week.

In terms of science we say it is a secondary sexual characteristic, but viewed in the light of the spirit of the whole, what is it except a song of praise and thanksgiving—joy in life, joy in the day, joy in the mate and brood, joy in the paternal and maternal instincts and solicitudes, a voice from the heart of nature that the world is good, thanksgiving for the universal beneficence without which you and I and the little bird would not be here? In foul weather as in fair, the bird sings. The rain and the cold do not silence him.

There are few or no pessimists among the birds. One might think the call of the turtle-dove, which sounds to us like "woe, woe, woe," a wail of despair; but it is not. It really means "love, love, love." The plaint of the wood pewee, pensive and like a human sigh, is far from pessimistic, although in a minor key. The cuckoo comes the nearest to being a pessimist, with his doleful call, and the catbird and the jay, with their peevish and complaining notes, might well be placed in that category, were it not for their songs when the love passion makes optimists even of them. The strain of the hermit thrush which floats down to me from the wooded heights above day after day at all hours, but more as the shades of night are falling—what does this pure, serene, exalted strain mean but that, in Browning's familiar words,

> God's in his heaven—
> All's right with the world!

The bird may sing for his mate and his brood alone, but what puts it into his heart to do that? Certainly it is good to have a mate and a brood!

A new season brings new experiences with the same old familiar birds, or new thoughts about them. This season I have had new impressions of our cuckoos, which are oftener heard than seen. Of the two species, the black-billed and the yellow-billed, the former prevails in the latitude of New England, and the latter farther south. We cannot hail our black-billed as "blithe newcomer," as Wordsworth does his cuckoo. "Doleful newcomer" would be a fitter title. There is nothing cheery or animated in his note, and he is about as much a "wandering voice" as is the European bird. He does not babble of sunshine and of flowers. He is a prophet of the rain, and the country people call him the rain crow. All his notes are harsh and verge on the weird. His nesting-instincts seem to lead him, or rather her, to the thorn-bushes as inevitably as the grass finch's lead her to the grass.

The cuckoo seems such an unpractical and inefficient bird that it is interesting to see it doing things. One of our young poets has a verse in which he sings of

> The solemn priestly bumble-bee
> That marries rose to rose.

He might apply the same or similar adjectives to the cuckoo. Solemn and priestly, or at least monkish, it certainly is. It is a real recluse and suggests the druidical. If it ever frolics or fights, or is gay and cheerful like our other birds, I have yet to witness it.

During the last summer, day after day I saw one of the birds going by my door toward the clump of thorn-trees with a big green worm in its bill. One afternoon I followed it. I found the bird sitting on a branch very still and straight, with the worm still in its beak. I sat down on the tentlike thicket and watched him. Presently he uttered that harsh, guttural note of alarm or displeasure. Then after a minute or two he began to shake and bruise the worm. I waited to see him disclose the nest, but he would not, and finally devoured the worm. Then he hopped or flitted about amid the branches above me, uttering his harsh note every minute or two.

After a half-hour or more I gave it up and parted the curtain of thorny branches which separated the thicket from the meadow and stepped outside. I had moved along only a few paces when I discovered the nest on an outer branch almost in the sunshine. The mother bird was covering her half-grown young. As I put up my hand toward her, she slipped off, withdrew a few feet into the branches, and uttered her guttural calls.

In the nest were four young, one of them nearly ready to leave it, while another barely had its eyes open; the eldest one looked frightened, while the youngest lifted up its head with open mouth for food. The most mature one pointed its bill straight up and sat as still as if petrified. The whole impression one got from the nest and its contents was of something inept and fortuitous. But the cares of a family woke the parents up and they got down to real work in caring for their charge.

The young had a curious, unbirdlike aspect with threadlike yellow stripes, and looked as if they were wet or just out of the shell.

That strain of parasitism in the blood of the cuckoo—how long in the history of its race since it mastered it and became its own nest-builder? But a crude and barbarous nest-builder it certainly is. Its "procreant cradle" is built entirely of the twigs of the thorn-tree, with all their sharp needle-like spines upon them, some of the twigs a foot long, bristling with spines, certainly the most forbidding-looking nest and nursery I ever beheld—a mere platform of twigs about four inches across, carpeted with a little shredded brown fibrous material, looking as if made from the inner bark of some tree, perhaps this very thorn.

In the total absence of the tent caterpillar or apple-tree worm, which is their favorite food, cuckoos seem to succeed in finding a large green worm here in the orchard. In the beech woods they can find a forest worm that is riddling the leaves of the beeches. The robins are there in force and I hope the cuckoos will join them in the destruction of the worms. It is interesting to see the cuckoo fly by several times a day with a big green worm in its beak. Inefficient as it seems, here it is doing things. It is like seeing a monk at the plough-handle. It is a solemn creature; its note is almost funereal.

Our indigo bunting is as artful and secretive about its nesting-habits as any of the sparrows. The male bird seems to know that his brilliant color makes him a shining mark, and he keeps far away from the nest, singing at all hours of the day in a circle around it, the radius of which must be more than fifty yards. In one instance the nest was near the house, almost under the clothes-line, in a low blackberry-bush, partly masked by tall-growing daisies and timothy. I chanced to pass near it, when off went the little brown bird with her sharp, chiding manners. She is a very emphatic creature. It is yea and nay with her every time.

The male seems like a bit of the tropics. He is not a very pleasing singer, but an all-day one and an all-summer one. He is one of our rarer birds. In a neighborhood where you see scores of sparrows and goldfinches you will see only one pair of indigobirds. Their range of food is probably very limited. I have never chanced to see them taking food of any kind.

How crowded with life every square rod of the fields and woods is, if we look closely enough! Beneath my leafy canopy on the edge of the beech woods where I now and then seek refuge from a hot wave, reclining on a cushion of dry leaves or sitting with my back against a cool, smooth exposure of the outcropping place rock, I am in a mood to give myself up to a day of little things. And the little things soon come trooping or looping along.

I see a green measuring-worm taking the dimensions of the rim of my straw hat which lies on the dry leaves beside me. It humps around it in an aimless sort of way, stopping now and then and rearing up on its hind legs and feeling the vacant space around it as a blind man might hunt for a lost trail. I know what it wants: it is on its travels looking for a place in which to go through that wonderful transformation of creeping worm into a winged creature. In its higher stage of being it is a little silvery moth, barely an inch across, and, like other moths, has a brief season of life and love, the female depositing its eggs in some suitable place and then dying or falling a victim to the wood pewee or some other bird. After some minutes of groping and humping about on my hat and on dry twigs and leaves, it is lost to my sight.

A little later a large black worm comes along. It is an inch and a quarter long, and is engaged in the same quest as its lesser brother of the green, transparent coat. Magnify it enough times, say, many thousand times, and what a terrible-looking monster we should have—a traveling arch of contracting and stretching muscular tissue, higher than your head, and measuring off the ground a rod or more at a time, or standing twenty feet or more high, like some dragon of the prime. But now it is a puny insect of which the caroling vireo overhead would quickly dispose.

With a twig I lift it to a maple sapling close by and watch it go looping up the trunk. Evidently it doesn't know just where it wants to go, but it finally strikes a small sugar maple and humps up that. By chance it strikes one of the branches six feet from the ground and goes looping up that. Then, by chance, in its aimless reachings it hits one of three small branches and climbs that a foot or more, and a dry twig, six or eight inches long, is seized and explored. At the end of it the creature tarries a minute or more, reaching out in the empty space, then turns back and hits a smaller twig on this twig about an inch long. This it explores over and over and sounds the depths that surround it, then loops back again to the end of the main twig it has just explored, profiting nothing by experience; then retraces its steps and measures off another small branch, and is finally lost to sight amid the leaves.

Has the course of life up through geologic time been in any way like this? There has been the push of life, the effort to get somewhere, but has there been no more guiding principle than in the case of this worm? The singular thing about the worm is its incessant reachings forth into surrounding space, searching, searching, sounding, sounding, as if to be sure that no chance to make a new connection is missed.

Finally the black worm comes to rest and, clinging by its hind feet, lets itself down and simulates a small dry twig, in which disguise it would deceive the sharpest-eyed enemy. No doubt it passed the night posing as a twig.

Among the sylvan denizens that next came upon the stage were a hummingbird, a little red newt, and a wood frog. The hummer makes short work of everything: with a flash and a hum it is gone. This one seemed to be exploring the dry twigs for nesting-material, either spiders' webs or bits of lichen. For a brief moment it perched on a twig a few yards from me. My ardent wish could not hold it any longer. Truly a fairy bird, appearing and vanishing like a thought, familiar with the heart of all the flowers and taking no food grosser than their nectar, the winged jewel of the poets, the surprise and delight of all beholders—it came like a burnished meteor into my leafy alcove and was gone as quickly.

All sylvan things have a charm and delicacy of their own, all except the woodchuck; wherever he is, he is of the earth earthy. The wood frog is known only to woodsmen and farm boys. He is a real sylvan frog, as pretty as a bird, the color of the dry leaves, slender and elegant in form and quick and furtive in movement. My feet disturbed one in the bed of dry leaves. Slowly I moved my hand toward him and stroked his back with a twig. If you can tickle a frog's back in any way you put a spell upon him. He becomes quite hypnotized. He was instantly responsive to my passes. He began to swell and foreshorten, and when I used my finger instead of the twig, he puffed up very rapidly, rose up more upon his feet, and bowed his head. As I continued the titillation he began to give forth broken, subdued croaks, and I wondered if he were going to break out in song. He did not, but he seemed loath to go his way. How different he looked from the dark-colored frogs which in large numbers make a multitudinous croaking and clucking in the little wild pools in spring! He wakes up from his winter nap very early and is in the pools celebrating his nuptials as soon as the ice is off them, and then in two or three days he takes to the open woods and assumes the assimilative coloring of the dry leaves.

The little orange-colored salamander, a most delicate and highly colored little creature, is as harmless as a baby, and about as slow and undecided in its movements. Its cold body seems to like the warmth of your hand. Yet in color it is as rich an orange as the petal of the cardinal flower is a rich scarlet. It seems more than an outside color; it is a glow, and renders the creature almost transparent, an effect as uniform as the radiance of a precious stone. Its little, innocent-looking, three-toed foot, or three and a half toed—how unreptilian it looks through my pocket glass! A baby's hand is not more so. Its throbbing throat, its close-shut mouth, its jet-black eyes with a glint of gold above them —only a close view of these satisfies one.

Here is another remarkable transformation among the small wild folk. In the spring he is a dark, slimy, rather forbidding lizard in the pools; now he is more beautiful than the jewel-weed in the woods. This is said to be an immature form, which returns to the ponds and matures the next season; but whether it is the male or the female that assumes this bright hue, or both, I do not know. The coat seems to be its midsummer holiday uniform which is laid aside when it goes back to the marshes to hibernate in the fall.

Wild creatures so unafraid are sure to have means of protection that do not at once appear. In the case of the newt it is evidently an acrid or other disagreeable secretion, which would cause any animal to repent that took it in its mouth. It is even less concerned at being caught than is the skunk, or porcupine, or stink-bug.

In my retreat I was unwittingly intruding upon the domain of another sylvan denizen, the chipmunk. One afternoon one suddenly came up from the open field below me with his pockets full of provender of some sort; just what sort I wondered, as there was no grain or seeds or any dry food that it would be safe to store underground for the winter.

Beholding me sitting there within two yards of his den was a great surprise to him. He eyed me a long time—squirrel time—making little, spasmodic movements on the flat stone above his den. At a motion of my arm he darted into his hole with an exultant chip. He was soon out with empty pockets, and he then proceeded to sound his little tocsin of distrust or alarm so that all the sylvan folk might hear. As I made no sign, he soon ceased and went about his affairs.

All this time, behind and above me, concealed by a vase fern, reposed that lovely creature of the twilight, the luna moth, just out of her chrysalis, drying and inflating her wings. I chanced to lift the fern screen, and there was this marvel! Her body was as white and spotless as the snow, and her wings, with their Nile-green hue, as fair and delicate as—well, as only those of a luna moth can be. It is as immaculate as an angel. With a twig I carefully lifted her to the trunk of a maple sapling, where she clung and where I soon left her for the night.

While I was loitering there on the threshold of the woods, observing the small sylvan folk, about a hundred yards above me, near the highway, was a bird's nest of a kind I had not seen for more than a score of years, the nest of the veery, or Wilson's thrush. Some friends were camping there with their touring-car outfit in a fringe of the beech woods, and passed and repassed hourly within a few yards of the nest, and, although they each had sharp eyes and sharp ears, they had neither seen nor heard the birds during the two days they had been there.

While calling upon them I chanced to see the hurried movements of a thrush in the low trees six or seven yards away. The bird had food in its beak, which caused me to keep my eye upon it. It quickly flew down to a small clump of ferns that crowned a small knoll in the open, about ten feet from the border of the woods. As it did so, another thrush flew out of the ferns and disappeared in the woods. Their stealthy movements sent a little thrill through me, and I said, Here is a treasure. I parted the ferny screen, and there on the top of the small knoll was the nest with two half-fledged young.

A mowing-machine in a meadow in front of my door gave an unkind cut to a sparrow that had a nest in the clover near the wall. The mower chanced to see the nest before the sickle-bar had swept over it. It contained four young ones just out of the shell. At my suggestion the mower carefully placed it on the top of a stone wall. The parent birds were not seen, but we naturally reasoned that they would come back and would alight upon the wall to make observations.

But that afternoon and the next morning passed, and we saw no anxious bird parents. The young lifted up their open mouths whenever I looked into the nest and seemed to be more contented than abandoned birds usually are. The next night was unseasonably cold, and I expected to find the nestlings dead in the morning; but they were not, and, strangely enough, for babes in the wood or rather on a stone wall, they seemed to be doing well. Maybe the mother bird is still caring for them, I said to myself, and I ambushed myself across the road opposite to them and watched.

I had not long to wait. The mother sparrow came slyly up and dropped some food into an open mouth and disappeared.

Who does not feel a thrill of pleasure when, in sauntering through the woods, his hat just brushes a vireo's nest? This was my experience one morning. The nest was like a natural growth, hanging there like a fairy basket in the fork of a beech twig, woven of dry, delicate, papery, brown and gray wood products, just high enough to escape prowling ground enemies and low enough to escape sharp-eyed tree enemies. Its safety was in its artless art. It was a part of the shadows and the green-and-brown solitude. The weaver had bent down one of the green leaves and made it a part of the nest; it was like the stroke of a great artist. Then the dabs of white here and there, given by the fragments of spiders' cocoons—all helped to blend it with the flickering light and shade.

I gently bent down the branch and four confident heads with open mouths instantly appeared above the brim. The mother bird meanwhile was flitting about in the branches overhead, peering down upon me and uttering her anxious "quay quay," equivalent, I suppose, to saying: "Get away!" This I soon did.

Most of our bird music, like our wild flowers, is soon quickly over. But the red-eyed vireo sings on into September—not an ecstatic strain, but a quiet, contented warble, like a boy whistling at his work.

VII

WITH ROOSEVELT AT PINE KNOT

It was in May during the last term of his Presidency that Roosevelt asked me to go with him down to Pine Knot, Virginia, to help him name his birds. I stayed with him at the White House the night before we started. I remember that at dinner[1] there was an officer from the British army stationed in India, and the talk naturally turned on Indian affairs. I did not take part in it because I knew nothing about India, but Roosevelt was so conversant with Indian affairs and Indian history that you would think he had just been cramming on it, which I knew very well he had not. But that British officer was put on his mettle to hold his own. In fact, Roosevelt knew more about India and England's relation to it than the officer seemed to know. It was amazing to see the thoroughness of his knowledge about India.

1 Mr. Burroughs's memory played him false here. The incident he speaks of was at a dinner in the White House, just before starting on the Yellowstone trip, in 1903. C. B.

The next morning we started off for Virginia, taking an early train.

Pine Knot is about one hundred miles from Washington. I think we left the train at Charlottesville, Virginia, and drove about ten miles to Pine Knot; the house is a big barnlike structure on the edge of the woods, a mile from the nearest farmhouse.

Before we reached there we got out of the wagon and walked, as there were a good many warblers in the trees—the spring migration was on. It was pretty warm; I took off my overcoat and the President insisted on carrying it. We identified several warblers there, among them the black-poll, the black-throated blue, and Wilson's black-cap. He knew them in the trees overhead as quickly as I did.

We reached Pine Knot late in the afternoon, but as he was eager for a walk we started off, he leading, as if walking for a wager. We went through fields and woods and briers and marshy places for a mile or more, when we stopped and mopped our brows and turned homeward without having seen many birds.

Mrs. Roosevelt took him to task, I think, when she saw the heated condition in which we returned, for not long afterwards he came to me and said: "Oom John, that was no way to go after birds; we were in too much of a hurry." I replied, "No, Mr. President, that isn't the way I usually go a-birding." His thirst for the wild and the woods, and his joy at returning to these after his winter in the White House, had evidently urged him on. He added, "We will try a different plan to-morrow."

So on the morrow we took a leisurely drive along the highways. Very soon we heard a wren which was new to me. "That's Bewick's wren," he said. We got out and watched it as it darted in and out of the fence and sang.

I asked him if he knew whether the little gray gnatcatcher was to be seen there. I had not seen or heard it for thirty years. "Yes," he replied, "I saw it the last time I was here, over by a spring run."

We walked over to some plum-trees where there had been a house at one time. No sooner had we reached the spot than he cried, "There it is now!" And sure enough, there it was in full song—a little bird the shape of a tiny catbird, with a very fine musical strain.

As we were walking in a field we saw some birds that were new to me. Roosevelt also was puzzled to know what they were till we went among them and stirred them up, discovering that they were females of the blue grosbeak, with some sparrows which we did not identify.

In the course of that walk he showed me a place where he had seen what he had thought at the time to be a flock of wild pigeons. He described how they flew, the swoop of their movements, and the tree where they alighted. I was skeptical, for it had long been thought that wild pigeons were extinct, but that fact had not impressed itself upon his mind. He said if he had known there could be any doubt about it, he would have observed them more closely. I was sorry that he had not, as it was one of the points on which I wanted indisputable evidence. We talked with the colored coachman about the birds, as he also had seen them. His description agreed with Roosevelt's, and he had seen wild pigeons in his youth; still I had my doubts. Subsequently Roosevelt wrote me that he had come to the conclusion that they had been mistaken about their being pigeons.

One day while there, as we were walking through an old weedy field, I chanced to spy, out of the corner of my eye, a nighthawk sitting on the ground only three or four yards away. I called Roosevelt's attention to it and said, "Now, Mr. President, I think with care you can drop your hat over that bird." So he took off his sombrero and crept up on the bird, and was almost in a position to let his hat drop over it when the bird flew to a near tree, alighting lengthwise on the branch as this bird always does. Roosevelt approached it again cautiously and almost succeeded in putting his hand upon it; the bird flew just in time to save itself from his hand.

One Sunday after church he took me to a field where he had recently seen and heard Lincoln's sparrow. We loitered there, reclining upon the dry grass for an hour or more, waiting for the sparrow, but it did not appear.

During my visit there we named over seventy-five species of birds and fowl, he knowing all of them but two, and I knowing all but two. He taught me Bewick's wren and the prairie warbler, and I taught him the swamp sparrow and one of the rarer warblers; I think it was the pine warbler. If he had found the Lincoln sparrow again, he would have been one ahead of me.

I remember talking politics a little with him while we were waiting for the birds, and, knowing that he was expecting Taft to be his successor, I expressed my doubts as to Taft's being able to fill his shoes.

"Oh, yes, he can," he said confidently; "you don't know him as well as I do."

"Of course not," I admitted; "but my feeling is that, though Taft is an able and amiable man, he is not a born leader."

(I am glad to say that Mr. Taft's recent course in support of the proposed League of Nations has quite brought me around to Roosevelt's estimate of him.)

Pine Knot is a secluded place in the woods. One evening as we sat in the lamplight, he reading Lord Cromer on Egypt, and I a book on the man-eating lions of Tsavo, and Mrs. Roosevelt sitting near with her needlework, suddenly Roosevelt's hand came down on the table with such a bang that it made us both jump, and Mrs. Roosevelt exclaimed in a slightly nettled tone, "Why, my dear, what *is* the matter?"

He had killed a mosquito with a blow that would almost have demolished an African lion.

It occurred to me later that evening how risky it was for the President of the United States to be so unprotected—without a guard of any kind—in that out-of-the-way place, and I expressed something of this to him, suggesting that some one might "kidnap" him.

"Oh," he answered, slapping his hand on his hip pocket, "I go armed, and they would have to be mighty quick to get the drop on me."

Shortly after that, to stretch my legs a little and listen to the night sounds in the Virginia woods, I went out around the cabin and almost immediately heard some animal run heavily through the woods not far from the house. I thought perhaps it was a neighboring dog, but, on speaking of it to Mrs. Roosevelt, was told that two secret service men came every night at nine o'clock and stood on guard till morning, spending the day at a farmhouse in that vicinity. She did not let the President know of this because it would irritate him.

The only flower we saw there which was new to me was the Indian pink. Roosevelt seemed to know the flowers as well as he did the birds. Pink moccasin-flowers and the bird's-foot violet were common in that locality.

On our return trip, Roosevelt's secretary being on the train, Roosevelt threw himself into the dictation of many letters, the wrens and the warblers already sidetracked for the business of the Administration.

I passed another night at the White House, and in the morning early we went out on the White House grounds to look for birds, our quest seeming to attract the puzzled attention of the passers-by.

"They often stare at me as though they thought me crazy," he said, "when they see me gazing up into the trees."

"Well, now they will think I am your keeper," I said.

"Yes, and I your nurse," laughed Mrs. Roosevelt.

When I left, Roosevelt gave me a list of the birds that we had seen while at Pine Knot and hoped that I would sometime write up the trip; in fact, for years after, whenever we would meet, almost the first thing he would say was, "Have you written up our Pine Knot trip yet, Oom John?" And his disappointment at my failure to do so was always unmistakable.[2]

2 The following letter may be of interest in this connection.
C. B.
DEAR OOM JOHN:
Did you ever get the pamphlet on Concealing Coloration? If not, I will send you another. I do hope that you will include in your coming volume of sketches a little account of the time you visited us at Pine Knot, our little Virginia camp, while I was President. I am very proud of you, Oom John, and I want the fact that you were my guest when I was President, and that you and I looked at birds together, recorded there—and don't forget that I showed you the blue grosbeak and the Bewick's wren, and almost all the other birds I said I would!

Ever yours,

THEODORE ROOSEVELT

VIII

A STRENUOUS HOLIDAY

One August a few years ago (1918) I set out with some friends for a two weeks' automobile trip into the land of Dixie—joy-riders with a luxurious outfit calculated to be proof against any form of discomfort.

We were headed for the Great Smoky Mountains in North Carolina. I confess that mountains and men that do not smoke suit me better. Still I can stand both, and I started out with the hope that the great Appalachian range held something new and interesting for me. Yet I knew it was a risky thing for an octogenarian to go a-gypsying, and with younger men. Old blood has lost some of its red corpuscles, and does not warm up easily over the things that moved one so deeply when one was younger. More than that, what did I need of an outing? All the latter half of my life has been an outing, and an "inning" seemed more in order. Then, after fourscore years, the desire for change, for new scenes and new people, is at low ebb. The old and familiar draw more strongly. Yet I was fairly enlisted and bound to see the Old Smokies.

Pennsylvania is an impressive State, so vast, so diversified, so forest-clad—the huge unbroken Alleghany ranges with their deep valleys cutting across it from north to south; the world of fine farms and rural homesteads in the eastern half, and the great mining and manufacturing interests in the western, the source of noble rivers; and the storehouse of many of Nature's most useful gifts to man.

The great Lincoln Highway, of course, follows the line of least resistance, but it has some formidable obstacles to surmount, and it goes at them very deliberately; and, in a powerful car, gives one a sense of easy victory. But I smile as I remember persons with lighter cars standing beside them at the foot of those long, winding ascents, nursing and encouraging them, as it were, and preparing them for the heavy task before them. An almost perfect road, worthy of its great namesake, but an Alleghany range which you cannot get around or through gives the automobilist pause.

As we were hurled along over the great highway the things I remember with the most satisfaction were the groups or processions of army trucks we met coming east. The doom of kaiserism was written large on that Lincoln Highway in that army of resolute, slow-moving army trucks. Dumb, khaki-colored fighters on wheels, staunch, powerful-looking, a host of them, rolling eastward toward the seat of war, some loaded with soldiers, some with camp equipments, and all hinting of the enormous resources the fatuous Kaiser had let loose upon himself in this far-off land. On other highways the weapons and materials of war were converging toward the great seaports in the same way. The silent, grim, processions—how impressive they were!

Pittsburgh is a city that sits with its feet in or very near the lake of brimstone and fire, and its head in the sweet country air of the hill-tops. I think I got nearer the infernal regions there than I ever did in any other city in this country. One is fairly suffocated at times driving along the public highway on a bright, breezy August day. It might well be the devil's laboratory. Out of such blackening and blasting fumes comes our civilization. That weapons of war and of destructiveness should come out of such pits and abysses of hell-fire seemed fit and natural, but much more comes out of them—much that suggests the pond-lily rising out of the black slime and muck of the lake bottoms.

We live in an age of iron and have all we can do to keep the iron from entering our souls. Our vast industries have their root in the geologic history of the globe as in no other past age. We delve for our power, and it is all barbarous and unhandsome. When the coal and oil are all gone and we come to the surface and above the surface for the white coal, for the smokeless oil, for the winds and the sunshine, how much more attractive life will be! Our very minds ought to be cleaner. We may never hitch our wagons to the stars, but we can hitch them to the mountain streams, and make the summer breezes lift our burdens. Then the silver age will displace the iron age.

The western end of Pennsylvania is one vast coal-mine. The farmer has only to dig into the side of the hill back of his house and take out his winter's fuel. I was surprised to see how smooth and gentle and grassy the hills looked. It is a cemetery of the old carboniferous gods, and it seems to have been prepared by gentle hands and watched over with kindly care. Good crops of hay and grain were growing above their black remains, and rural life seemed to go on in the usual way. The shuffling and the deformation of the earth's surface which attended the laying down of the coal-beds is not anywhere evident. The hand of that wonderful husbandman, Father Time, has smoothed it all out.

Our first camp was at Greensborough, thirty or more miles southeast of Pittsburgh, an ideal place—a large, open oak grove on a gentle eminence well carpeted with grass, with wood and water in abundance. But the night was chilly. Folding camp-cots are poor conservers of one's bodily warmth, and until you get the hang of them and equip yourself with plenty of blankets, Sleep enters your tent very reluctantly. She tarried with me but briefly, and at three or four in the morning I got up, replenished the fire, and in a camp-chair beside it indulged in the "long, long thoughts" which belong to age much more than to youth. Youth was soundly and audibly sleeping in the tents with no thoughts at all.

The talk that first night around the camp-fire gave us an inside view of many things about which we were much concerned. The ship question was the acute question of the hour and we had with us for a few days Commissioner Hurley, of the Shipping Board, who could give us first-hand information, which he did to our great comfort.

Our next stop was near Uniontown, Pennsylvania, where for that night we slept indoors.

On the following day one of the big cars had an accident—the fan broke, and the iron punctured the radiator. It looked as if we should be delayed until a new radiator could be forwarded from Pittsburgh. We made our way slowly to Connellsville, where there was a good garage, but the best workmen there shook their heads; they said a new radiator was the only remedy. All four arms of the fan were broken off and there was no way to mend them. This verdict put Mr. Ford on his mettle. "Give me a chance," he said, and, pulling off his coat and rolling up his sleeves, he fell to work. In two hours we were ready to go ahead. By the aid of drills and copper wire the master mechanic had stitched the severed arms to their stubs, soldered up the hole in the radiator, and the disabled car was again in running order.

On August the 31st we made our camp on the banks of a large, clear creek in West Virginia called Horseshoe Run. A smooth field across the road from the creek seemed attractive, and I got the reluctant consent of the widow who owned it to pitch our camp there, though her patch of roasting-ears near by made her hesitate; she had probably had experiences with gypsy parties, and was not impressed in our favor even when I gave her the names of two well-known men in our party. But Edison was not attracted by the widow's open field; the rough, grassy margin of the creek suited him better, and its proximity to the murmuring, eddying, rocky current appealed to us all, albeit it necessitated our mess-tent being pitched astride a shallow gully, and our individual tents elbowing one another in the narrow spaces between the boulders. But wild Nature, when you can manage her, is what the camper-out wants. Pure elements—air, water, earth—these settle the question; Camp Horseshoe Run had them all. It was here, I think, that I got my first view of the nonpareil, or painted bunting—a bird rarely seen north of the Potomac.

An interesting object near our camp was an old, unused grist-mill, with a huge, decaying overshot oaken water-wheel. We all perched on the wheel and had our pictures taken.

At our lunch that day, by the side of a spring, a twelve-year-old girl appeared in the road above us with a pail of apples for sale. We invited her into our camp, an invitation she timidly accepted. We took all of her apples. I can see her yet with her shining eyes as she crumpled the new one-dollar bill which one of the party placed in her hand. She did not look at it; the feel of it told the story to her. We quizzed her about many things and got straight, clear-cut answers—a very firm, level-headed little maid. Her home was on the hill above us. We told her the names of some of the members of the party, and after she had returned home we saw an aged man come out to the gate and look down upon us. An added interest was felt whenever we came in contact with any of the local population. Birds and flowers and trees and springs and mills were something, but human flowers and rills of human life were better. I do not forget the other maiden, twelve or thirteen years old, to whom we gave a lift of a few miles on her way. She had been on a train five times, and once had been forty miles from home. Her mother was dead and her father lived in Pennsylvania, and she was living with her grandfather. When asked how far it was to Elkins she said, "Ever and ever so many miles."

The conspicuous roadside flowers for hundreds of miles, in fact, all the way from Pennsylvania to North Carolina, were the purple eupatorium, or Joe-Pye-weed, and the ironweed—stately, hardy growths, and very pleasing to look upon, the ironweed with its crimson purple, and the eupatorium with its massive head of soft, pinkish purple.

August the 22d we reached Cheat River in West Virginia, a large, clear mountain trout-brook. It crossed our path many times that day. Every mountain we crossed showed us Cheat River on the other side of it. It was flowing by a very devious course northwest toward the Ohio. We were working south and east.

We made our camp that night on the grounds of the Cheat Mountain Club, on the banks of the river—an ideal spot. The people at the big clubhouse gave us a hospitable welcome and added much to our comfort. I found the forests and streams of this part of West Virginia much like those of the Catskills, only on a larger scale, and the climate even colder. That night the mercury dropped to thirty. On June the 24th they had a frost that killed all their garden truck. The paper outlines of big trout which covered the walls in the main room of the clubhouse told the story of the rare sport the club-members have there. Evidently Cheat River deserves a better name.

The mountains and valleys of the Virginias all present a marked contrast to those of New York and Pennsylvania. They were not rubbed down and scooped out by the great ice-sheet that played such a part in shaping our northern landscapes. The valleys are markedly V-shaped, while ours are markedly U-shaped. The valley sides are so steep that they are rarely cultivated; the farm land for the most part lies on the tops of the broad, rounded hills, though we passed through some broad, open river valleys that held miles upon miles of beautiful farms in which hay and oats were still being harvested. Everywhere were large fields of buckwheat, white with bloom, and, I presume, humming with bees.

Here and there, by the rocks and the boulders strewn over the landscape, I saw evidences of large local glaciers that had hatched in these mountains during the great Ice Age.

We made camp at Bolar Springs on August the 23d—a famous spring, and a beautiful spot. We pitched our tents among the sugar maples, and some of the party availed themselves of the public bathhouse that spanned the overflow of the great spring. The next night our camp was at Wolf Creek, not far from the Narrows—a beautiful spot, marred only by its proximity to the dusty highway. It was on the narrow, grassy margin of a broad, limpid creek in which the fish were jumping. Some grazing horses disturbed my sleep early in the morning, but on the whole I have only pleasant memories of our camp at Wolf Creek.

We were near a week in Virginia and West Virginia, crossing many times the border between the two States, now in one, then in the other, all the time among the mountains, with a succession of glorious views from mountain-tops and along broad, fertile valleys. Now we were at Warm Springs, then at Hot Springs, then at White Sulphur, or at Sweet Water Springs. Soft water and hard water, cold water and warm water, mineral water and trout-streams, companion one another in these mountains. This part of the continent got much folded and ruptured and mixed up in the building, and the elements are unevenly distributed.

I think to most of us West Virginia had always been a rather hazy proposition, and we were glad to get a clear impression of it. We certainly became pretty intimate with the backbone of the continent—or with its many backbones, as its skeleton seems to be a very multiplex affair. The backbones of continents usually get broken in many places, but they serve their purpose just as well. In fact, our old Earth is more like an articulate than a vertebrate. Its huge shell is in many sections.

One of our camps we named Camp Lee, the name of the owner of the farm. One of the boys there, Robert E. Lee, made himself very useful in bringing wood and doing other errands.

A privation, which I think Mr. Edison and I felt more than did the others, was the scanty or delayed war news; the local papers, picked up here and there, gave only brief summaries, and when in the larger towns we could get some of the great dailies, the news was a day or two old. When one has hung on the breath of the newspapers for four exciting years, one is lost when cut off from them.

Such a trip as we were taking was, of course, a kind of a lark, especially to the younger members of the party. Upon Alleghany Mountain, near Barton, West Virginia, a farmer was cradling oats on a side-hill below the road. Our procession stopped, and the irrepressible Ford and Firestone were soon taking turns at cradling oats, but with doubtful success. A photograph shows the farmer and Mr. Ford looking on with broad smiles, watching Mr. Firestone with the fingers of the cradle tangled in the oats and weeds, a smile on his face also, but decidedly an equivocal smile—the trick was not so easy as it looked. Evidently Mr. Ford had not forgotten his cradling days on the home farm in Michigan.

Camp-life is a primitive affair, no matter how many conveniences you have, and things of the mind keep pretty well in the background. Occasionally around the camp-fire we drew Edison out on chemical problems, and heard formula after formula come from his lips as if he were reading them from a book. As a practical chemist he perhaps has few, if any, equals in this country. It was easy to draw out Mr. Ford on mechanical problems. There is always pleasure and profit in hearing a master discuss his own art.

A plunge into the South for a Northern man is in many ways a plunge into the Past. As soon as you get into Virginia there is a change. Things and people in the South are more local and provincial than in the North. For the most part, in certain sections, at least, the county builds the roads (macadam), and not the State. Hence you pass from a fine stone road in one county on to a rough dirt road in the next. Toll-gates appear. In one case we paid toll at the rate of two cents a mile for the cars, and five cents for the trucks. Grist-mills are seen along the way, driven by overshot wheels, and they are usually at work. A man or a boy on horseback, with a bag of grain or of meal behind him, going to or returning from the mill, is a frequent sight; or a woman on horseback, on a sidesaddle, with a baby in her arms, attracts your attention. Thus my grandmother went to mill in pioneer days in the Catskills.

The absence of bridges over the small streams was to us a novel feature. One of the party called these fording places, "Irish bridges." They are made smooth and easy, and gave us no trouble. Another Southern feature, indicating how far behind our Northern and more scientific farming the South still is, are the groups of small haystacks in the meadows with poles sticking out of their tops, letting the rain and the destructive bacteria into their hearts. Among the old-fashioned features of the South much to be commended are the large families. In a farmhouse near which we made camp one night there were thirteen children, the eldest of whom was at the front in France. The schools were in session in late August, and the schoolrooms were well filled with pupils.

No doubt there are many peculiar local customs of which the hurrying tourist gets no inkling. At a station in the mountains of North Carolina a youngish, well-clad countryman, smoking his pipe, stood within a few feet of my friend and me and gazed at us with the simple, blank curiosity of a child. There was not the slightest gleam of intelligent interest, or self-consciousness in his face; it was the frank stare of a five-year-old boy. He belongs to a type one often sees in the mountain districts of the South—good human stuff, valiant as soldiers, and industrious as farmers, but so unacquainted with the great outside world, their unsophistication is shocking to see.

It often seemed to me that we were a luxuriously equipped expedition going forth to seek discomfort, for discomfort in several forms—dust, rough roads, heat, cold, irregular hours, accidents—is pretty sure to come to those who go a-gypsying in the South. But discomfort, after all, is what the camper-out is unconsciously seeking. We grow weary of our luxuries and conveniences. We react against our complex civilization, and long to get back for a time to first principles. We cheerfully endure wet, cold, smoke, mosquitoes, black flies, and sleepless nights, just to touch naked reality once more.

Our two chief characters presented many contrasts: Mr. Ford is more adaptive, more indifferent to places, than is Mr. Edison. His interest in the stream is in its potential water-power. He races up and down its banks to see its fall, and where power could be developed. He never ceases to lament so much power going to waste, and points out that if the streams were all harnessed, as they could easily be, farm labor everywhere, indoors and out, could be greatly lessened. He dilates upon the benefit that would accrue to every country neighborhood if the water-power that is going to waste in its valley streams were set to work in some useful industry, furnishing employment to the farmers and others in the winter seasons when the farms need comparatively little attention. He is always thinking in terms of the greatest good to the greatest number. He aims to place his inventions within reach of the great mass of the people. As with his touring-car, so with his tractor engine, he has had the same end in view. Nor does he forget the housewife. He has plans afoot for bringing power into every household that will greatly lighten the burden of the women-folk.

Partly owing to his more advanced age, but mainly, no doubt, to his meditative and introspective cast of mind, Mr. Edison is far less active than is Mr. Ford. When we would pause for the midday lunch, or to make camp at the end of the day, Mr. Edison would sit in his car and read, or curl up, boy fashion, under a tree and take a nap, while Mr. Ford would inspect the stream or busy himself in getting wood for the fire. Mr. Ford is a runner and a high kicker, and frequently challenged some of the party to race with him. He is also a persistent walker, and from every camp, both morning and evening, he sallied forth for a brisk half-hour walk. His cheerfulness and adaptability on all occasions, and his optimism in regard to all the great questions, are remarkable. His good-will and tolerance are boundless. Notwithstanding his practical turn of mind, and his mastery of the mechanical arts and of business methods, he is through and through an idealist. As tender as a woman, he is much more tolerant. He looks like a poet, and conducts his life like a philosopher. No poet ever expressed himself through his work more completely than Mr. Ford has expressed himself through his car and his tractor engine. They typify him; not imposing, nor complex, less expressive of power and mass than of simplicity, adaptability, and universal service, they typify the combination of powers and qualities which make him a beneficent, a likable, and a unique personality. Those who meet him are invariably drawn to him. He is a national figure, and the crowds that flock around the car in which he is riding, as we pause in the towns through which we pass, are not paying their homage merely to a successful car-builder or business man, but to a beneficent human force, a great practical idealist whose good-will and spirit of universal helpfulness they have all felt. He has not only brought pleasure and profit into their lives, but has illustrated and written large upon the pages of current history a new ideal of the business man—that of a man whose devotion to the public good has been a ruling passion, and whose wealth has inevitably flowed from the depth of his humanitarianism. He has taken the people into partnership with him, and has eagerly shared with them the benefits that are the fruit of his great enterprise—a liberator, an emancipator, through channels that are so often used to enslave or destroy.

In one respect, essentially the same thing may be said of Mr. Edison: his first and leading thought has been, "What can I do to make life easier and more enjoyable to my fellow-men? He is a great chemist, a trenchant and original thinker on all the great questions of life, though he has delved but little into the world of art and literature—a practical scientist, plus a meditative philosopher of profound insight. And his humor is delicious. We delighted in his wise and witty sayings. A good camper-out, he turns vagabond very easily, can go with hair disheveled and clothes unbrushed as long as the best of us, and can rough it week in and week out and wear that benevolent smile. He eats so little that I think he was not tempted by the chicken-roosts or turkey-flocks along the way, nor by the cornfields and apple-orchards, as some of us were, but he is second to none in his love for the open and for wild nature.

Mr. Firestone belongs to an entirely different type—the clean, clear-headed, conscientious business type; always on his job, always ready for whatever comes; in no sense an outdoor man; always at the service of those around him; a man generous, kindly, appreciative, devoted to his family and his friends; sound in his ideas—a manufacturer who has faithfully and honestly served his countrymen.

It is after he gets home that a meditative man really makes such a trip. All the unpleasant features are strained out or transformed. In retrospect it is all enjoyable, even the discomforts. I am aware that I was often irritable and ungracious, but my companions were tolerant, and gave little heed to the flitting moods of an octogenarian. Now, at this distance, and sitting beside my open fire at Slabsides, I look upon the whole trip with unmixed pleasure.

IX

UNDER GENIAL SKIES

I. A SUN-BLESSED LAND

The two sides of our great sprawling continent, the East and West, differ from each other almost as much as day differs from night. On the coast of southern California the dominant impression made upon one is of a world made up of three elements—sun, sea, and sky. The Pacific stretches away to the horizon like a vast, shining, gently undulating floor. Its waves are longer and come in more languidly than they do upon the Atlantic coast. It justifies its name. The passion and fury of the Eastern seas I got no hint of, even in winter. Its rocks, all that I saw of them, are soft and friable. The languid waves rapidly wear them down. They are non-strenuous rocks, lifted up out of a non-strenuous sea. The mountains that tower four or five thousand feet along the coast are of the same character. They are young, and while they carry their heads very high, they are soft and easily disintegrated compared with the granite of our coast.

As a rule, young mountains always wear the look of age, from their deep lines and jagged and angular character, while the really old mountains wear the look of youth from their comparative smoothness, their unwrinkled appearance, their long, flowing lines. Time has taken the conceit all out of them.

The annual rainfall in the Far West is only about one third of what it is on the eastern side of the continent. And the soil is curiously adapted to the climate. Trees flourish and crops are grown there under arid conditions that would kill every green thing on the Atlantic seaboard. The soil is clay tempered with a little sand, probably less than ten per cent of it by weight is sand. I washed the clay out of a large lump of it and found the sand a curious heterogeneous mixture of small and large, light and dark grains of all possible forms. The soil does not bake as do our clay soils, and keeps moist when ours would almost defy the plough. Under cultivation it works up into a good tillable condition. Its capacity to retain moisture is remarkable, as if it were made for a scant rainfall. As a crop-producing soil, it has virtues which I am at a loss to account for. Root vegetables grown here have a sweetness, and above all, a tenderness, of which we know nothing in the East. Much sunshine in our climate makes root vegetables fibrous and tough.

I more than half believe that the wonderful sweetness of the bird songs here, such as that of the meadowlark, is more or less a matter of climate; the quality of the sunshine seems to have affected their vocal cords. The clear, piercing, shaft-like note of our meadowlark contrasts with that of the Pacific variety as our hard, brilliant blue skies contrast with the softer and tenderer skies of this sun-blessed land.

II. LAWN BIRDS

To have a smooth grassy lawn about your house on the Pacific coast is to have spread out before you at nearly all hours of the day a pretty spectacle of wild-bird life. Warblers, sparrows, thrushes, titlarks, and plovers flutter across it as thick as autumn leaves—not so highly colored, yet showing a pleasing variety of tints, while the black ph[oe]be flits about your porch and arbor vines.

Audubon's warbler is the most numerous, probably ten to one of any other variety of birds. Then the white-crowned sparrows, Gambel's sparrow, the tree sparrow, and one or two other sparrows of which I am not sure are next in number.

Two species of birds from the Far North are usually represented by a solitary specimen of each, namely, the Alaska hermit thrush and the American pipit, or titlark. The thrush is silent, but has its usual trim, alert look. The pipit is the only walker in the group. It walks about like our oven-bird with the same pretty movement of the head and a teetering motion of the hind part of the body.

While in Alaska, in July, 1899, with the Harriman Expedition, I found the nest of the pipit far up on the side of a steep mountain. It was tucked in under a mossy tuft and commanded a view of sea and mountain such as Alaska alone can afford.

But the most conspicuous and interesting of all these lawn birds are the ring-necked plovers, or killdeers. Think of having a half-dozen or more of those wild, shapely creatures, reminiscent of the shore and of the spirit of the tender, glancing April days, running over your lawn but a few yards from you! Their dovelike heads, their long, slender legs, that curious, mechanical jerking up-and-down movement of their bodies, their shrill, disconsolate cries as they take flight, their beautiful and powerful wings and tail, and their mastery of the air—all arrest your attention or challenge your admiration. They bring the distant and the furtive to your very door. All climes and lands wait upon their wings. They fly around the world.

The plovers are the favored among birds. Beauty, speed, and immunity from danger from birds of prey are theirs. Ethereal and aerial creatures! Is that the cry of the sea in the bird's voice? Is that the motion of the waves in its body? Is that the restlessness of the surf in its behavior?

However high and far it may fly, it has to come back to earth as we all do. It comes to our lawn to feed upon earthworms. The other birds are all busy picking up some minute fly or insect that harbors in the grass, but the plover is here for game that harbors in the turf. His methods are like those of the robin searching for grubs or angle-worms. He scrutinizes the turf very carefully as he runs about over it, making frequent drives into it with his bill, but only now and then seizing the prey of which he is in search. When he does so, he shows the same judgment which the robin does under like conditions. He pulls slowly and evenly, so as to make sure of the whole worm, or to compel it to let go its hold upon the soil without breaking. All birds are wise about their food-supplies.

On the beach the wild life that I see is all on wings. There are the tranquil, effortless gliding herring gulls, snow-white beneath and pearl-gray above, displaying an affluence of wing-power restful to look upon—airplanes that put forth their powers so subtly and so silently as to elude both eye and ear. At low tide I see large groups of their white and gray-blue forms seated upon the dark, moss-covered rocks. Fresh water is at a premium on this coast, and the thirsty gulls avail themselves of the makeshift of the drain-pipes from the town, which discharge on the beach.

There are the clumsy-looking but powerful-winged birds, the brown pelicans, usually in a line of five or six, skimming low over the waves, shaping their course to the "hilly sea," often gliding on set wings for a long distance, rising and falling to clear the water—coasting, at it were, on a horizontal surface, and only at intervals beating the air for more power. They are heavy, awkward-looking birds with wings and forms that suggest none of the grace and beauty of the usual shore birds. They do not seem to be formed to cleave the air, or to part the water, but they do both very successfully. When the pelican dives for his prey, he is for the moment transformed into a thunderbolt. He comes down like an arrow of Jove, and smites and parts the water in superb style. When he recovers himself, he is the same stolid, awkward-looking creature as before.

A bird evidently not far removed from its reptilian ancestors—a bird that is at home under the water and hunts its prey there on the wing—is the black cormorant. There is a colony of several hundred of them on the face of a sea-cliff a short distance above me.

I see, at nearly all hours of the day, the black lines they make above the foaming breakers as they go and come on their foraging expeditions. In diving, they disappear under the water like the loon, and penetrate to as great depths. One does not crave an intimate acquaintance with them, but they are interesting as a part of the multitudinous life of the shore.

III. SILKEN CHAMBERS

The trap-door spider has furnished me with one of the most interesting bits of natural history I have found on the coast. An obliging sojourner near me from one of the Eastern States had discovered a large plot of uncultivated ground above the beach that abounded in the hidden burrows of these curious animals. One afternoon he volunteered to conduct me to the place.

The ground was scantily covered with low bushy and weedy growths. My guide warned me that the quarry we sought was hard to find. I, indeed, found it so. It not only required an "eye as practiced as a blind man's touch," it required an eye practiced in this particular kind of detective work. My new friend conducted me down into the plot of ground and, stopping on the edge of it, said, "There is a nest within two feet of me." I fell to scrutinizing the ground as closely as I knew how, fairly bearing on with my eyes; I went over the soil inch by inch with my eyes, but to no purpose. There was no mark on the gray and brown earth at my feet that suggested a trap-door, or any other device. I stooped low, but without avail. Then my guide stooped, and with a long needle pried up a semicircular or almost circular bit of the gray soil nearly the size of a silver quarter of a dollar, which hinged on the straight side of it, and behold—the entrance to the spider's castle! I was not prepared for anything so novel and artistic—a long silken chamber, about three quarters of an inch in diameter, concealed by a silken trap-door, an inch in its greatest diameter. The under side of the door, a dull white, the color of old ivory, is slightly convex, and its top is a brownish gray to harmonize with its surroundings, and slightly concave. Its edges are beveled so that it fits into the flaring or beveled end of the chamber with the utmost nicety. No joiner could have done it better. A faint semicircular raised line of clay as fine as a hair gave the only clue. The whole effect, when the door was held open, was of a pleasing secret suddenly revealed.

Then we walked about the place, and, knowing exactly what to look for, I gave my eyes another chance, but they were slow to profit by it. My guide detected one after another, and when I failed, he would point them put to me. But presently I caught on, as they say, and began to find them unaided.

We often found the lord of the manor on duty as doorkeeper, and in no mood to see strangers. He held his door down by inserting his fangs in two fine holes near the edge and bracing himself, or, rather, herself (as, of course, it is the female), offered a degree of resistance surprising in an insect. If one persists with a needle, there is often danger of breaking the door. But when one has made a crack wide enough to allow one to see the spider, she lets go her hold and rushes farther down in her burrow.

Occasionally we found one about half the usual size, indicating a young spider, but no other sizes. My guide said they only emerge from their tunnel at night, and proved it by an ingenious mechanical device made of straws attached to the door. When the door was opened, the straws lifted up, but did not fall down when it was closed. Whenever he found the straw still up in the morning he knew the door had been opened in the night.

As they are nocturnal in habits, they doubtless prey upon other insects, such as sow-bugs and crickets, which the night brings forth. Two bright specks upon the top of the head appear to be eyes, but they are so small they probably only serve to enable them to tell night from day. I think these spiders are mainly guided by a marvelously acute tactile sense. They probably feel the slightest vibration in the earth or air, unless they have a sixth sense of which we know nothing.

All their work, the building and repairing of their nests, as well as all their hunting, is done by night. This habit, in connection with their extreme shyness, makes the task of getting at their life-histories a difficult one. The inside of the burrow seems coated with a finer and harder substance than the soil in which they are dug. It is made on the spot, the spider mixing some secretion of her own with the clay, and working it up into a finer product.

The trap-door sooner or later wears out at the hinge, and is then discarded and a new door manufactured. We saw many nests with the old door lying near the entrance. The door is made of several layers of silk and clay, and is a substantial affair.

The spider families all have the gift of genius. Of what ingenious devices and arts are they masters! How wide their range! They spin, they delve, they jump, they fly. They are the original spinners. They have probably been on their job since carboniferous times, many millions of years before man took up the art. And they can spin a thread so fine that science makes the astonishing statement that it would take four millions of them to make a thread the caliber of one of the hairs of our head—a degree of delicacy to which man can never hope to attain.

Trap-doors usually mean surprises and stratagems, secrets and betrayals, and this species of the arachnids is proficient in all these things.

The adobe soil on the Pacific coast is as well fitted to the purposes of this spider as if it had been made for her special use. But, as in all such cases, the soil was not made for her, but she is adapted to it. It is radically unlike any soil on the Atlantic coast—the soil for cañons and the rectangular watercourses, and for the trap-door spider. It is a tough, fine-grained homogeneous soil, and when dry does not crumble or disintegrate; the cohesion of particles is such that sun-dried brick are easily made from it.

This spider is found in New Mexico, Arizona, California, and Jamaica. It belongs to the family of *Mygalidae*. It resembles in appearance the tarantula of Europe, described by Fabre, and has many of the same habits; but its habitation is a much more ingenious and artistic piece of workmanship than that of its European relative. The tarantula has no door to her burrow, but instead she builds about the entrance a kind of breastwork an inch high and nearly two inches in diameter, and from this fortress sallies out upon her prey. She sinks a deeper shaft than does our spider, but excavates it in the same way with similar tools, her fangs, and lines it with silk from her own body.

Our spider is an artist, evidently the master builder and architect of her kind. Considering her soft and pussy-like appearance—no visible drills for such rough work—one wonders how she excavates a burrow six inches or more deep in this hard adobe soil of the Pacific coast, and how she removes the dirt after she has loosened it. But she has been surprised at her work; her tools are her two fangs, the same weapons with which she seizes and dispatches her prey, and the rake or the *chelicerœ*. To use these delicate instruments in such coarse work, says Fabre, seems as "illogical as it would to dig a pit with a surgeon's scalpel." And she carries the soil out in her mandibles, a minute pellet at a time, and drops it here and there at some distance from her nest.

Her dooryard is never littered with it. It takes her one hour to dig a hole the size of half an English walnut, and to remove the earth.

One afternoon I cut off the doors from two nests and left them turned over, a few inches away. The next morning I found that the occupants of the nests, under cover of the darkness, had each started the construction of a new door, and had it about half finished. It seemed as if the soil on the hinge side had begun to grow, and had put out a semicircular bit of its surface toward the opposite side of the orifice, each new door copying exactly the color of the ground that surrounded it, one gray from dead vegetable matter, the other a light brick-red. I read somewhere of an experimenter who found a nest on a mossy bit of ground protectively colored in this way. He removed the lid and made the soil bare about. The spider made a new lid and covered it with moss like the old one, and her art had the opposite effect to what it had in the first case. This is typical of the working of the insect mind. It seems to know everything, and yet to know nothing, as we use the term "know."

On the second morning, one of the doors had attained its normal size, but not yet its normal thickness and strength. It was much more artfully concealed than the old one had been. The builder had so completely covered it with small dry twigs about the size of an ordinary pin, and had so woven these into it, standing a few of them on end, that my eye was baffled. I knew to an inch where to look for the door, and yet it seemed to have vanished. By feeling the ground over with a small stick I found a yielding place which proved to be the new unfinished door. Day after day the door grew heavier and stronger. The builder worked at it on the under side, adding new layers of silk. There is always a layer of the soil worked into the door to give it weight and strength.

Spiders, like reptiles, can go months without food. The young, according to Fabre, go seven months without eating. They do not grow, but they are very active; they expend energy without any apparent means of keeping up the supply. How do they do it? They absorb it directly from the sun, Fabre thinks, which means that here is an animal between which and the organic world the vegetable chlorophyl plays no part, but which can take at first-hand, from the sun, the energy of life. If this is true, and it seems to be so, it is most extraordinary.

In view of the sex of the extraordinary spider I have been considering, it is interesting to remember that one difference between the insect world and the world of animal life to which we belong, which Maeterlinck has forgotten to point out, is this:

In the vertebrate world, the male rules; the female plays a secondary part. In the insect world the reverse is true. Here the female is supreme and often eats up the male after she has been fertilized by him. Motherhood is the primary fact, fatherhood the secondary. It is the female mosquito that torments the world. It is the female spider that spins the web and traps the flies. Size, craft, and power go with the female. The female spider eats up the male after he has served her purpose; her caresses mean death. The female scorpion devours the male in the same way. Among our wild bees it is the queen alone that survives the winter and carries on the race. The big noisy blow-flies on the window-pane are females. With the honey bees the males are big and loud, but are without any authority, and are almost as literally destroyed by the female as is the male spider. The queen bee does not eat her mate, but she disembowels him. The work of the hive is done by the neuters. In the vertebrate world it is chiefly among birds of prey that the female is the larger and bolder; the care of the young devolves largely upon her. Yes, there is another exception: Among the fishes, the females are, as a rule, larger than the males; the immense number of eggs which they carry brings this about.

There are always exceptions to this dominance of the female in the insect world. We cannot corner Nature and keep her cornered. She would not be Nature if we could. With the fireflies, it is the male that dominates; the female is a little soft, wingless worm on the ground, always in the larval state.

In the plant world, also, the male as a rule is dominant. Behold the showy catkins of the chestnuts, the butternuts, the hazelnuts, the willows, and other trees. The stamens of most flowers are numerous and conspicuous. Our Indian corn carries its panicle of pollen high above the silken tresses which mother the future ear.

One day I dug up a nest which was occupied by a spider with her brood of young ones. I took up a large block of earth weighing ten pounds or more, and sank it in a box of earth of its own kind. I kept it in the house under observation for a week, hoping that at some hour of day or night the spider would come out. But she made no sign. My ingenious friend arranged the same mechanical contrivance over the door which he had used successfully before. But the latch was never lifted. Madam Spider sulked or bemoaned her fate at the bottom of her den. At the end of a week I broke open the nest and found her alone. She had evidently devoured all her little ones.

I kept two nests with a spider in each in the house for a week, and in neither case did the occupant ever leave its nest.

Apparently the young spiders begin to dig nests of their own when they are about half-grown. As to where they stay, or how they live up to that time, I have no clue. The young we found in several nests were very small, not more than an eighth of an inch long. Of the size and appearance of the male spider, and where he keeps himself, I could get no clue.

One morning I went with my guide down to the spider territory, and saw him try to entice or force a spider out of her den. The morning previous he had beguiled several of them to come up to the opening by thrusting a straw down the burrow and teasing them with it till in self-defense they seized it with their fangs and hung on to it till he drew them to the surface. But this morning the trick would not work. Not one spider would keep her hold. But with a piece of wire bent at the end in the shape of a hook, he finally lifted one out upon the ground. How bright and clean and untouched she looked! Her limbs and a part of the thorax were as black as jet and shone as if they had just been polished. No lady in her parlor could have been freer from any touch of soil or earth-stain than was she. On the ground, in the strong sunlight, she seemed to be lost. We turned her around and tried to induce her to enter the nest again; but over and over she ran across the open door without heeding it. In the novel situation in which she suddenly found herself, all her wits deserted her, and not till I took her between my thumb and finger and thrust her abdomen into the hole, did she come to herself. The touch of that silk-lined tube caused the proper reaction, and she backed quickly into it and disappeared.

Just what natural enemy the trap-door spider has I do not know. I never saw a nest that had been broken into or in any way disturbed, except those which we had disturbed in our observations.

I often wonder what mood of Nature this world of cacti which we run against in the great Southwest expresses. Certainly something savage and merciless. To stab and stab again suits her humor. How well she tempers her daggers and bayonets! How hard and smooth and sharp they are! How they contrast with the thick, succulent stalks and leaves which bear them! It is a desert mood; heat and drought appear to be the exciting causes. The scarcity of water seems to stimulate Nature to store up water in vegetable tissues, just as it stimulates men to build great dams and reservoirs. These giant cacti are reservoirs of water. But why spines and prickles and cruel bayonets? They certainly cannot be for protection or defense; the grass and other vegetation upon which the grazing animals feed are not armed with spines.

If the cacti were created that grazing animals in the desert might have something to feed upon, as our fathers' way of looking at things might lead us to believe, why was that benevolent plan frustrated by the armor of needles and spines?

Nature reaches her hungry and thirsty creatures this broad, mittened hand like a cruel joke. It smites like a serpent and stings like a scorpion. The strange, many-colored, fascinating desert! Beware! Agonies are one of her garments.

All we can say about it is that Nature has her prickly side which drought and heat aggravate. In the North our thistles and thorns and spines are a milder expression of this mood. The spines on the blackberry-bush tend against its propagation for the same reason. Among our wild gooseberries, there are smooth and prickly varieties, and one succeeds about as well as the other. Apple-and pear-trees in rough or barren places that have a severe struggle for life, often develop sharp, thorny branches. It is a struggle of some kind which begets something like ill-temper in vegetation—heat and drought in the desert, and browsing animals and poor soil in the temperate zones. The devil's club in Alaska is one mass of spines; why, I know not. It must just be original sin. Our raspberries have prickles on their stalks, but the large, purple-flowering variety is smooth-stemmed.

Mr. John C. Van Dyke in his work on the desert expresses the belief that thorns and spines are given to the desert plants for protection; and that if no animal were there that would eat them, they would not have these defenses. But I believe if there had never been a browsing animal in the desert the cacti would have had their thorns just the same.

Nature certainly arms her animal forms against one another. We know the quills of the porcupine are for defense, and that the skunk carries a weapon that its enemies dread, but I do not believe that any plant form is armed against any creature whose proper food it might become. Cacti carry formidable weapons in the shape of spines and thorns, but the desert conditions where they are found, heat and aridity, are no doubt their primary cause. The conditions are fierce and the living forms are fierce.

We cannot be dogmatic about Nature. From our point of view she often seems partial and inconsistent. But I would just as soon think that Nature made the adobe soil in the arid regions that the human dwellers there might have material at hand with which to construct a shelter, as that she gives spines and daggers to any of the vegetable forms to secure their safety. One may confute Mr. Van Dyke out of his own mouth. He says:

Remove the danger which threatened the extinction of a family, and immediately Nature removes the defensive armor. On the desert, for instance, the yucca has a thorn like a point of steel. Follow it from the desert to the high tropical table-lands of Mexico where there is plenty of soil and moisture, plenty of chance for yuccas to thrive, and you will find it turned into a tree and the thorn merely a dull blade-ending. Follow the sahuaro and the pitahaya into the tropics again, and with their cousin, the organ cactus, you will find them growing a soft thorn that would hardly penetrate clothing.

But are they not just as much exposed to browsing animals in the high table-lands as in the desert, if not more so?

Mr. Van Dyke asserts that Nature is more solicitous about the species than about the individual. She is no more solicitous about the one than the other. The same conditions apply to all. But the species are numerous; a dozen units may be devoured while a thousand remain. A general will sacrifice many soldiers to save his army, he will sacrifice one man to save ten, but Nature's ways are entirely different. Both contending armies are hers, and she is equally solicitous about both. She wants the cacti to survive, and she wants the desert animals to survive, and she favors both equally. All she asks of them is that they breed and multiply endlessly. Notwithstanding, according to Van Dyke, Nature has taken such pains to protect her desert plants, he yet confesses that, although it seems almost incredible, it is nevertheless true that "deer and desert cattle will eat the cholla—fruit, stem, and trunk—though it bristle with spines that will draw blood from the human hand at the slightest touch."

This question of spines and thorns in vegetation is a baffling one because Nature's ways are so unlike our ways. Darwin failed utterly in his theory of the origin of species, because he proceeded upon the idea that Nature selects as man selects. You cannot put Nature into a formula.

Behold how every branch and twig of our red thorn bristles with cruel daggers! But if they are designed to keep away bird or beast from eating its fruit, see how that would defeat the tree's own ends! If no creature ate its little red apples and thus scattered its seeds, the fruit would rot on the ground beneath the branches, and the tribe of red thorns would not increase. And increase alone is Nature's end.

It is safe to say, as a general statement, that the animal kingdom is full of design. Every part and organ of our bodies has its purpose which serves the well-being of the whole. I do not recall any character of bird or beast, fish or insect, that does not show purpose, but in the plant world Nature seems to allow herself more freedom, or does not work on so economical a plan. What purpose do the spines on the prickly ash serve? or on the thistles? or on the blackberry, raspberry, gooseberry bushes? or the rose? Our purple-flowering raspberry has no prickles, and thrives as well as any. The spines on the blackberry and raspberry do not save them from browsing cattle, nor their fruit from the birds. In fact, as I have said, the service of the birds is needed to sow their seeds. The devil's club of Alaska is untouchable, it is so encased in a spiny armor; but what purpose the armor serves is a mystery. We know that hard conditions of soil and climate will bring thorns on seedling pear-trees and plum-trees, but we cannot know why.

The yucca or Spanish bayonet and the century-plant, or American aloe (*Agave americana*), are thorny and spiny; they are also very woody and fibrous; yet nothing eats them or could eat them. They are no more edible than cordwood or hemp ropes. This fact alone settles the defense question about spines.

V. SEA-DOGS

There is a bit of live natural history out here in the sea in front of me that is new and interesting. A bunch of about a dozen hair seals have their rendezvous in the unstable waves just beyond the breakers, and keep together there week after week. To the naked eye they seem like a group of children sitting there on a hidden bench of rock, undisturbed by the waves that sweep over them. Their heads and shoulders seem to show above the water, and they appear to be having a happy time.

Now and then one may be seen swimming about or lifted up in a wall of green-blue transparent water, or leaping above the wrinkled surface in the exuberance of its animal spirits. I call them children of the sea, until I hear their loud barking, and then I think of them as dogs or hounds of the sea. Occasionally I hear their barking by night when it has a half-muffled, smothered sound.

They are warm-blooded, air-breathing animals, and there seems something incongruous in their being at home there in the cold briny deep—badgers or marmots that burrow in the waves, wolves or coyotes that hunt their prey in the sea.

Their progenitors were once land animals, but Darwinism does not tell us what they were. The whale also was once a land animal, but the testimony of the rocks throws no light upon its antecedents. The origin of any new species is shrouded in the obscurity of whole geological periods, and the short span of human life, or of the whole human history, gives us no adequate vantage-ground from which to solve the problem.

I can easily believe that these hair seals are close akin to the dog. They have five digits; they bolt their food like dogs; their sense of smell is said to be very acute, though how it could serve them in the sea does not appear. The young are born upon the land and enter the water very reluctantly.

This seal is easily tamed. It has the intelligence of the dog and attaches itself to its master as does the dog. Its sense of direction and locality is very acute. This group of seals in front of me, day after day, and week after week, returns to the same spot in the ever-changing waters, without the variation of a single yard, so far as I can see. The locality is purely imaginary. It is a love tryst, and it seems as if some sixth sense must guide them to it. Locality is as unreal in the sea as in the sky, but these few square yards of shifting waters seem as real to these seals as if they were a granite ledge. They keep massed there on the water at that particular point, with their flippers protruding above the surface, as if they were as free from danger as so many picnickers. Yet something attracts them to this particular place. I know of no other spot along the coast for a hundred miles or more where the seals congregate as they do here. What is the secret of it? Evidently it is a question of security from their enemies. At this point the waves break much farther out than usual, which indicates a hidden reef or bench of rocks, and comparatively shallow water. This would prevent their enemies, sharks and killer whales, from stealing up beneath them and pulling them down. I do not hear their barking in the early part of the night, but long before morning their half-muffled baying begins. Old fishermen tell me that they retire for the night to the broad belts of kelp that lie a hundred yards or more out to sea. Doubtless the beds of kelp also afford them some protection from their enemies. The fishermen feel very bitter toward them on account of the fish they devour, and kill them whenever opportunity offers. Often when I lie half asleep in the small hours of the morning, I seem to see these amphibian hounds pursuing their quarry on the unstable hills and mountains of the sea, and giving tongue at short intervals, as did the foxhounds I heard on the Catskills in my youth.

X

A SHEAF OF NATURE NOTES

The Spirit of the Hive, which Maeterlinck makes so much of, seems to give us the key to the psychic life of all the lower orders. What one knows, all of that kind seem to know at the same instant. It seems as if they drew it in with the air they breathed. It is something like community of mind, or unity of mind. Of course it is not an intellectual process, but an emotional process; not a thought, as with us, but an impulse.

So far as we know there is nothing like a council or advisory board in the hive. There are no decrees or orders. The swarm is a unit. The members act in concert without direction or rule. If anything happens to the queen, if she is lost or killed, every bee in the hive seems to know it at the same instant, and the whole swarm becomes greatly agitated. The division of labor in the hive is spontaneous: the bees function and coöperate as do the organs in our own bodies, each playing its part without scheme or direction.

This community of mind is seen in such an instance as that of the migrating lemmings from the Scandinavian peninsula. Vast hordes of these little creatures are at times seized with an impulse to migrate or to commit suicide, for it amounts to that. They leave their habitat in Norway and, without being deflected by any obstacle, march straight toward the sea, swimming lakes and rivers that lie in their way. When the coast is reached, they enter the water and continue on their course. Ship captains report sailing for hours through waters literally alive with them. This suicidal act of the lemmings strikes one as a kind of insanity. It is one of the most puzzling phenomena I know of in animal life. But the migration of all animals on a large scale shows the same unity of purpose. The whole tribe shares in a single impulse. The annual migration of the caribou in the North is an illustration. In the flocking birds this unity of mind is especially noticeable. The vast armies of passenger pigeons which we of an older generation saw in our youth moved like human armies under orders. They formed a unit. They came in countless hordes like an army of invasion, and they departed in the same way. Their orders were written upon the air; their leaders were as intangible as the shadows of their wings. The same is true of all our flocking birds; a flock of snow buntings, or of starlings, or of blackbirds, will act as one body, performing their evolutions in the air with astonishing precision.

In Florida, in the spring when the mating-instinct is strong, I have seen a flock of white ibises waltzing about the sky, going through various intricate movements, with the precision of dancers in a ballroom quadrille. No sign, no signal, no guidance whatever. Let a body of men try it under the same conditions, and behold the confusion, and the tumbling over one another! At one moment the birds would wheel so as to bring their backs in shadow, and then would flash out the white of their breasts and under parts. It was like the opening and shutting of a giant hand, or the alternate rapid darkening and brightening of the sail of a tacking ice-boat. This is the spirit of the flock. When a hawk pursues a bird, the birds tack and turn as if linked together. When one robin dashes off in hot pursuit of another, behold how their movements exactly coincide! The hawk-hunted bird often escapes by reaching the cover of a tree or a bush, but not by dodging its pursuer, as a rabbit or a squirrel will dodge a dog. Schools of fish act with the same machine-like unity.

In the South, I have seen a large area of water, acres in extent, uniformly agitated by a school of mullets apparently feeding upon some infusoria on the surface, and then instantly, as if upon a given signal, the fish would dive and the rippling cease. It showed a unity of action as of ten thousand spindles controlled by electricity.

How quickly the emotion of fear is communicated among the wild animals! How wild and alarmed the deer become after the opening of the first day of the shooting season. Those who have not seen or heard a hunter seem to feel the impending danger.

The great flocks of migrating butterflies (the monarch) illustrate the same law. In the fall they are all seized with this impulse to go South and thousands of them march in one body. At night they roost in the trees. I have seen photographs of them in which they appeared like a new kind of colored foliage covering the trees. In the return flight in the spring, the same massing again occurs. Recently the Imperial Valley in California was invaded by a vast army of worms moving from east to west. In countries that have been cursed with a plague of grasshoppers witnesses of the spectacle describe them as moving in the same way. They stopped or delayed railway trains and automobiles, their crushed bodies making the rails and highways as slippery as grease would have made them. Ten million or ten billion behaving as one.

This community of mind stands the lower orders in great stead. It makes up to them in a measure for the want of reason and judgment. In what we call telepathy we get hints of the same thing among ourselves. Telepathy is probably a survival from our earlier animal state.

II. MAETERLINCK ON THE BEE

Maeterlinck, in his "Life of the Bee" resists the conclusion of Sir John Lubbock that flies are more intelligent than honey bees:

> If you place in a bottle half a dozen bees [says Sir John], and the same number of flies, and lay the bottle down horizontally with its base to the window, you will find that the bees will persist till they die of exhaustion or hunger in their endeavors to discover an issue through the glass; while the flies, in less than two minutes, will all have sallied forth through the neck on the opposite side.

The flies are more intelligent than the bees because their problems of life are much more complicated; they are fraught with many more dangers; their enemies lurk on all sides; while the bees have very few natural enemies. There are no bee-catchers in the sense that there are scores of flycatchers. I know of no bird that preys upon the worker bees. The kingbird is sometimes called the "bee martin" because he occasionally snaps up the drones. All our insectivorous birds prey upon the flies; the swallows sweep them up in the air, the swifts scoop them in, while, besides the so-called flycatchers, the cedar-birds, the thrushes, the vireos, and all other soft-billed birds, subsist more or less upon them. Try to catch a big blow-fly upon the window-pane and see how difficult the trick is, while with a honey bee it is no trick at all. Or try to "swat" the ordinary house-fly with your hand. See how he squares himself and plants himself as your threatening hand approaches! He is ready for a trial of speed. He seems to know that your hand is slower than he is, and he is right in most cases. Now try a honey bee. The case is reversed. The bee has never been stalked; it shows no fear; and to crush it is as easy as to crush a beetle.

The wit and cunning of all animals are developed by their struggle for existence. The harder the struggle, the more their intelligence. Our skunk and porcupine are very stupid because they do not have to take thought about their own safety; Nature has done that for them.

To bolster up his case, Maeterlinck urges that "the capacity for folly so great in itself argues intelligence," which amounts to saying that the more fool you are, the more you know.

Buffon did not share Maeterlinck's high opinion of the intelligence of the bee; he thought the dog, the monkey, and the majority of other animals possess far more; an opinion which I share. Indeed, of free intelligence the bee possesses very little. The slave of an overmastering instinct, as our new nature poet, McCarthy, says,

> She makes of labor an eternal lust.

Bees do wonderful things, but do them blindly. They work as well (or better) in the darkness as in the light. The Spirit of the Hive knows and directs all. The unit is the swarm, and not the individual bee.

The bee does not know fear; she does not know love. She will defend the swarm with her life, but her fellows she heeds not.

It is very doubtful if the individual bees of the same hive recognize one another at all outside the hive. Every beehunter knows how the bees from the same tree will clip and strike at one another around his box, when they are first attracted to it. After they are seriously engaged in carrying away his honey, they pay no attention to one another or to bees from other swarms.

That bees tell one another of the store of honey they have found is absurd. The unity of the swarm attends to that.

Maeterlinck tells of a little Italian bee that he once experimented upon during an afternoon, the results showing that this bee had told the news of her find to eighteen bees! Its "vocabulary" stood it in good stead!

Maeterlinck's conception of the Spirit of the Hive was an inspiration, and furnishes us with the key to all that happens in the hive. The secret of all its economies are in the phrase. Having hit upon this solution, he should have had the courage to stand by it. But he did not. He is continually forgetting it and applying to his problem the explanations we apply in our dealings with one another. He talks of the power of the bees to give "expression to their thoughts and feelings"; of their "vocabulary," phonetic and tactile; he says that the "extraordinary also has a name and place in their language"; that they are able to "communicate to each other news of an event occurring outside the hive"; all of which renders his Spirit of the Hive superfluous. He quotes from a French apiarist who says that the explorer of the dawn,—the early bee,—like the early bird that catches the worm, returns to the hive with the news that "the lime-trees are blooming to-day on the banks of the canal"; "the grass by the roadside is gay with white clover"; "the sage and the lotus are about to open"; "the mignonette and the lilies are overflowing with pollen." Whereupon the bees must organize quickly and arrange to divide the work. They probably call a council of the wise ones and after due discussion and formalities proceed to send out their working expeditions. "Five thousand of the sturdiest will sally forth to the lime-trees, while three thousand juniors go and refresh the white clover." "They make daily calculations as to the means of obtaining the greatest possible wealth of saccharine liquid."

When Maeterlinck speaks of "the hidden genius of the hive issuing its commands," or recognizes the existence among the bees of spiritual communications that go beyond a mere "yes" or "no," he is true to his own conception.

The division of labor among hive bees is of course spontaneous, like all their other economies—not a matter of thought, but of instinct.

Maeterlinck and other students of the honey bee make the mistake of humanizing the bee, thus making them communicate with one another as we communicate. Bees have a language, they say; they tell one another this and that; if one finds honey or good pasturage, she tells her sisters, and so on. This is all wide of the mark. There is nothing analogous to verbal communication among the insects. The unity of the swarm, or the Spirit of the Hive, does it all. Bees communicate and coöperate with one another as the cells of the body communicate and coöperate in building up the various organs. The spirit of the body coördinates all the different organs and tissues, making a unit of the body.

If some outside creature, such as a mouse or a snail, penetrates into the hive, and dies there, the bees encase it in wax, or bury it where it lies, so that it cannot contaminate the hive, and a foreign object in the body, such as a bullet in the lungs, or in the muscles, becomes encysted in an analogous manner, and is thus rendered harmless.

Kill a bee in or near the hive and the smell of its crushed body will infuriate the other bees. But crush a bee in the fields or by the bee-hunter's box which is swarming with bees, and the units from the same hive heed it not.

Bees have no fear. They have no love or attachment for one another as animals have. If one of their number is wounded or disabled, they ruthlessly expel it from the hive. In fact, they belong to another world of beings that is absolutely oblivious of the world of which we form a part. They murder or expel the drones, after they have done their work of fertilizing the queen, in the most cruel and summary manner. Their apparent attachment to the queen, and their loyalty to her, are not personal. They do not love her. It is the Spirit of the Hive, or the cult of the swarm solicitous about itself. There are no brothers, sisters, fathers, mothers, among the bees; there are only co-workers, working not for the present, but for the future. When we enter the kingdom of the bee, we must leave all our human standards behind. These little people have no red blood, no organs of sense, as we have; they breathe and hear through their legs, their antennæ.

The drones do not know the queen as such in the hive. Their instincts lead them to search for her in the air during her nuptial flight, and they know her only there. The drones have thirteen thousand eyes, while the workers have only six thousand. This double measure of the power of vision is evidently to make sure that the males discover the queen in her course through the air.

The guards that take their stand at the gate, the bees that become fans at the entrance to ventilate the hive, the nurses, the bees that bring the bee-bread, the bees that pack it into the cells, the bees that go forth to find a home for the new swarm, the sweepers and cleaners of the hive, the workers that bring propolis to seal up the cracks and crevices—all act in obedience to the voiceless Spirit of the Hive.

After we have discounted Maeterlinck so far as the facts will bear us out in doing, it remains to be said that he is the philosopher of the insect world. If Fabre is the Homer, as he himself has said, Maeterlinck is the Plato of that realm. How wisely he speaks of the insect world in his latest volume, "Mountain Paths":

The insect does not belong to our world. The other animals, the plants even, notwithstanding their dumb life and the great secrets which they cherish, do not seem wholly foreign to us. In spite of all, we feel a certain earthly brotherhood with them. They often surprise and amaze our intelligence, but do not utterly upset it. There is something, on the other hand, about the insect that does not belong to the habits, the ethics, the psychology of our globe. One would be inclined to say that the insect comes from another planet, more monstrous, more energetic, more insane, more atrocious, more infernal than our own. One would think that it was born of some comet that had lost its course and died demented in space.

Speaking of the intelligence of bees reminds me of a well-known woodsman and camp-fire man who recently extolled in print the intelligence of hornets, saying that they have the ability to differentiate friends from foes. "They know us and we talk to them and they are made to feel as welcome as any of our guests." "When a stranger visits the camp, they attract the attention of one they know *who recognizes their signal by thought or gesture and leaves immediately, returning only when the stranger has departed.*" (The italics are mine.) He says the same hornets apparently come to them year after year, greeting them on their arrival, and, should they be accompanied by strangers, they treat them with the same deference as "when they visit us after we have been in camp some time."

Did one ever hear before of such well-bred and well-mannered bees? What would Maeterlinck say to all that? Its absurdity becomes apparent when we remember that hornets live but a single season, that none of them lives over the winter, save the queen, and that she never leaves the nest in summer after she has got her family of workers around her.

III. ODD OR EVEN

One of our seven wise men once said to me, "Have you observed that in the inorganic world things go by even numbers, and in the organic world by odd?" I immediately went down to the edge of a bushy and swampy meadow below our camp and brought him a four-petaled flower of galium, and a plant-stalk with four leaves in a whorl. In another locality I might have brought him dwarf cornel, or the houstonia, or wood-sorrel, or the evening-primrose. Yet even numbers are certainly more suggestive of mechanics than of life, while odd numbers seem to go more with the freedom and irregularity of growing things.

One may make pretty positive assertions about non-living things. Crystals, so far as I know, are all even-sided, some are six and some eight-sided; snowflakes are of an infinite variety of pattern, but the number six rules them. In the world of living things we cannot be so sure of ourselves. Life introduces something indeterminate and incommensurable. It makes use of both odd and even, though undoubtedly odd numbers generally prevail. Leaves that are in lobes usually have three or five lobes. But the stems of the mints are four-square, and the cells of the honey bee are six-sided. We have five fingers and five toes, though only four limbs. Locomotion is mechanical and even numbers serve better than odd. Hence the six-legged insects. In the inorganic world things attain a stable equilibrium, but in the living world the equilibrium is never stable. Things are not stereotyped, hence the danger of dogmatizing about living things. Growing Nature will not be driven into a corner.

Well may Emerson ask—

> Why Nature loves the number five,
> And why the star form she repeats?

The number five rules in all the largest floral families, as in the crowfoot family, the rose family (which embraces all our fruit trees), the geranium family, the flax family, the campanula family, the convolvulus family, the nightshade family. Then there is a large number of flowers the parts of which go in threes, one of the best known of which is the trillium. In animal life the starfish is the only form I recall based on the number five.

IV. WHY AND HOW

One may always expect in living nature variations and modifications. It is useless to ask why. Nature is silent when interrogated in this way. Ask her how, and you get some results. If we ask, for instance, why the sting of the honey bee is barbed, and those of the hornet and wasp and bumble-bee, and of other wild bees, are smooth like a needle, so that they can sting and sting again, and live to sting another day, while the honey bee stings once at the cost of its life; or why only one species of fish can fly; or why one kind of eel has a powerful electric battery; or why the porcupine has an armor of quills while his brother rodent the woodchuck has only fur and hair, and so on—we make no addition to our knowledge.

But if we ask, for instance, how so timid and defenseless an animal as the rabbit manages to survive and multiply, we extend our knowledge of natural history. The rabbit prospers by reason of its wakefulness—by never closing its eyes—and by its speed; also by making its home where it can command all approaches, and so flee in any direction. Or if we ask how our ruffed grouse survives and prospers in a climate where its cousin the quail perishes, we learn that it eats the buds of certain trees, while the quail is a ground-feeder and is often cut off by a deep fall of snow.

If we ask why the chipmunk hibernates, we get no answer; but if we ask how he does it, we find out that he stores up food in his den, hence must take a lunch between his naps. The woodchuck hibernates, also, but he stores up fuel in the shape of fat in his own body. The porcupine is above ground and active all winter. He survives by gnawing the bark of certain trees, probably the hemlock. We have two species of native mice that look much alike, the white-footed mouse and the jumping, or kangaroo, mouse. The white-foot is active the season through, over and under the snow; the jumper hibernates all winter, and apparently accomplishes the feat by the power he has of barely keeping the spark of life burning. His fires are banked, so to speak; his temperature is very low, and he breathes only at long intervals.

If, then, we ask with Emerson, "*why* Nature loves the number five," and "*why* the star form she repeats," we shall be put to it for an answer. We can only say that with living things odd numbers are more likely to prevail, and with non-living, even numbers.

Some seeds have wings and some have not. To ask why, is a blind question, but if we ask *how* the wingless seeds get sown, we may add to our knowledge.

In our own practical lives, in which experimentation plays such a part, we are often compelled to ask why this result and not that, why this thing behaves this way and that thing that way. We are looking for reasons or causes. The farmer asks why his planting in this field was a failure, while it was a success in the next field, and so on. An analysis of his soil or of his fertilizer and culture will give him the answer.

V. AN INSOLUBLE PROBLEM

That Darwin was a great natural philosopher and a good and wise man admits of no question, but to us, at this distance, it seems strange enough that he should have thought that he had hit upon the key to the origin of species in the slow and insensible changes which he fancied species underwent during the course of the geologic ages, and should thus have used the phrase as the title of his book. Had he called his work the "Variability of Species," or the "Modification of Species," it would not have been such a misnomer. Sudden mutations give us new varieties, but not new species. In fact, of the origin of species we know absolutely nothing, no more than we do about the origin of life itself.

Of the development of species we know some of the factors that play a part, as the influence of environment, the struggle for existence, and the competitions of life. But do we not have to assume an inherent tendency to development, an original impulse as the key to evolution? Accidental conditions and circumstances modify, but do not originate species. The fortuitous plays a part in retarding or hastening a species, and in its extinction, but not in its origin. The record of the rocks reveals to us the relation of species, and their succession in geologic time, but gives no hint of their origin.

Agassiz believed that every species of animal and plant was the result of a direct and separate act of the Creator. But the naturalist sees the creative energy immanent in matter. Does not one have to believe in something like this to account for the world as we see it? And to account for us also?—a universal mind or intelligence

> Whose dwelling is the light of setting suns,
> And the round ocean and the living air,
> And the blue sky, and in the mind of man.

Agassiz was too direct and literal; he referred to the Infinite Mystery in terms of our own wills and acts. When we think of a Creator and the thing created as two, we are in trouble at once. They are one, as fire and light are one, as soul and body are one. Darwin said he could not look upon the world as the result of chance, and yet his theory of the origin of species ushers us into a chance world. But when he said, speaking of the infinite variety of living forms about us, that they "have all been produced by laws acting around us," he spoke as a great philosopher. These laws are not fortuitous, or the result of the blind grouping of irrational forces.

VI. A LIVE WORLD

It was "the divine Kepler," as Professor Shaler calls him, who looked upon the earth as animated in the fashion of an animal. "To him this world is so endowed with activities that it is to be accounted alive." But his critics looked upon this fancy of Kepler's as proof of a disordered mind.

Now I read in a work of George Darwin's (son of the great naturalist) on the tides that the earth in many ways behaves more like a living organism than like a rigid insensate sphere. Its surface throbs and palpitates and quivers and yields to pressure as only living organisms do. The tides can hardly be regarded as evidences of its breathing, as Kepler thought they could, but they are proof of how closely it is held in the clasp of the heavenly forces. It is like an apple on the vast sidereal tree, that has mellowed and ripened with age. Our moon is no doubt as dead as matter can be. It is hard to fancy its surface yielding to our tread as does that of the earth. Then we know that the absence of air and water on it is proof that it cannot be endowed with what we call life. George Darwin tells us that when we walk on the ground we warp and bend the surface very much as we might bend or dent the epidermis of a colossal pachyderm. He and his brother devised an instrument by which the slight fluctuations of the ground, as we move over it, could be measured. The instrument was so delicate that it revealed the difference of effect produced by the same pressure at seven feet and at six feet from the instrument! More than that, the instrument revealed the throbbing and agitations which the ground is undergoing at all times. They found that minute earthquakes, or microseisms, as the Italians call them, are occurring constantly.

Another instrument has been invented called the microphone, which translates this earth's movements into sound—its tremors and agitations become audible. This microphone, when placed in a cave twenty feet below the surface, and carefully protected by means of a carpet from any accidental disturbance in its immediate vicinity, revealed what is called "natural telluric phenomena; such as roarings, explosions, occurring isolated or in volleys, and metallic or bell-like sounds." "The noises sometimes become intolerably loud," especially on one occasion in the middle of the night, half an hour before a sensible earthquake.

Our apparently impassive and slumbering old planet evidently has dreams we know little of.

From Professor Shaler's "Nature and Man in America" I get an impression which again deepens my feeling of something half human about our lucky planet, at least something progressive and unequal, like life itself. Shaler finds that organic development in the Northern Hemisphere is more advanced, by a whole geologic period, than in the Southern, with Europe at the head and Australia the greatest laggard. The animal life of Australia is much like that of Europe in the Jurassic period, while both Asia and Africa possess forms, such as elephants, and tigers, and lions, which abounded in Europe in Tertiary times. Hence the Northern Hemisphere is more like the head of the beast, and the Southern more like the viscera. The Northern races easily dominate the Southern. The flowering of civilization is in the North. It is very certain that man originated north of the equator. I think that one need not expect that the achievements of man in Australia, or in South America, will rival the achievements of man nearer the magnetic pole of the earth.

VII. DARWINISM AND THE WAR

That Darwinism was indirectly one of the causes of the World War seems to me quite obvious. Unwittingly the great and gentle naturalist has more to answer for than he ever dreamed of. His biological doctrine of the struggle for existence, natural selection, and the survival of the fittest, fairly intoxicated the Germans from the first. These theories fell in well with their militarism and their natural cruelty and greediness. Their philosophers took them up eagerly. Weissmann fairly made a god of natural selection, as did other German thinkers. And when they were ready for war, the Germans at once applied the law of the jungle to human affairs. The great law of evolution, the triumph of the strong, the supremacy of the fit, became the foundation of their political and national ideals. They looked for no higher proof of the divinity of this law, as applied to races and nations, than the fact that the organic world had reached its present stage of development through the operation of this law. Darwin had given currency to these ideas. He had denied that there was any inherent tendency to development, affirming that we lived in a world of chance, and that power comes only to him who exerts power—half truths, all of them.

The Germans as a people have never been born again into the light of our higher civilization. They are morally blind and politically treacherous. Their biological condition is that of the lower orders, and the Darwinian law of progress came to them as an inspiration. Darwin's mind, in its absence of the higher vision, was akin to a German mind. In his plodding patience, his devotion to details, and in many other ways, his mind was German. But in his candor, his truthfulness, his humility, his simplicity, he was anything but German. Undoubtedly his teachings bore fruit of a political and semi-political character in the Teutonic mind. The Teutons incorporated the law of the jungle in their ethical code. Had not they the same right to expansion and to the usurpation of the territory and to the treasures of their neighbors that every weed in the fields and even the vermin of the soil and the air have? If they had the sanction of natural law, that was enough; they were quite oblivious to the fact that with man's moral nature had come in a new biological law which Darwin was not called upon to reckon with, but which has tremendous authority and survival value—the law of right, justice, mercy, honor, love.

We do not look for the Golden Rule among swine and cattle, or among wolves and sharks; we look for it among men; we look for honor, for heroism, for self-sacrifice, among men. None of these things are involved in the Darwinian hypothesis. There is no such thing as right or wrong in the orders below man. These are purely human distinctions. It is not wrong for the wolf to eat the lamb, or the lamb to eat the grass, but an aggressive war is wrong to the depths of the farthest star. Germany's assault upon the peace and prosperity of the world was a crime against the very heavens.

Darwin occupied himself only with the natural evolution of organic forms, and not with the evolution of human communities. He treated man as an animal, and fitted him into the zoölogical scheme. He removed him from the realm of the miraculous into the plane of the natural. For all purposes of biological discussion, man is an animal, but that is not saying he is only an animal, and still under the law of animal evolution. The European man is supposed to have passed the stage of savagery, in which the only rule of right is the rule of might. To have made Darwinism an excuse for a war of aggression is to have debased a sound natural philosophy to a selfish and ignoble end.

Germany lifted the law to the human realm and staked her all upon it, and failed. The moral sense of the world—the sense of justice, of fair play—was against her, and inevitably she went down. Her leaders were morally blind.

When the rest of the world talked of moral standards, the German leaders said, "We think you are fools." But these standards brought England into the war—the sacredness of treaties. They brought the United States in. We saw a common enemy in Germany, an enemy of mankind. We sent millions of men to France for an ideal—for justice and fair play. To see our standards of right and justice ignored and trampled upon in this way was intolerable. The thought of the world being swayed by Prussianism was unbearable. I said to myself from the first, "The Allies have got to win; there is no alternative." And what astonishes me is that certain prominent Englishmen, such as Lord Morley, and others, did not see it. Would they have sat still and watched Germany destroy France and plant herself upon the Channel and make ready to destroy England? The very framework of our moral civilization would have been destroyed. Darwin little dreamed to what his natural selection theory was to lead.

VIII. THE ROBIN

Of all our birds the robin has life in the fullest measure, or best stands the Darwinian test of the fittest to survive. His versatility, adaptiveness, and fecundity are remarkable. While not an omnivorous feeder, he yet has a very wide range among fruits and insects. From cherries to currants and strawberries he ranges freely, while he is the only thrush that makes angle-worms one of his dietetic staples and looks upon a fat grub as a rare tidbit. Then his nesting-habits are the most diverse of all. Now he is a tree-builder in the fork of a trunk or on a horizontal branch, then a builder in vines or rosebushes around your porch, then on some coign of vantage about your house or barn, or under the shed, or under a bridge, or in the stone wall, or on the ground above a hedge. I have known him to go into a well and build there on a projecting stone. He even nests beyond the Arctic Circle, and it is said he never sings sweeter than when singing during those long Arctic days.

He brings off his first brood in May, and the second in June, and if a dry season does not seriously curtail his food-supply, a third one in September. He is a hustler in every sense of the word—a typical American in his enterprise and versatility. His voice is the first I hear in the morning, and the last at night. Little wonder that there are twenty robins to one bluebird, or wood thrush, or catbird. The song sparrow is probably our next most successful bird, but she is far behind the robin. We could never have a plague of song sparrows or bluebirds, but since the robins are now protected in the South as well as in the North, we are exposed to the danger of a plague of robins. Since they may no longer have robin pot-pies in Mississippi, the time is near at hand when we may no longer have cherry-pies in New York or New England. Yet who does not cherish a deep love for the robin? He is a plebeian bird, but he adds a touch to life in the country that one would not like to miss.

The robin is neither a walker nor a hopper; he is doomed always to be a runner. Go slow he cannot; his engine is always "in high"—it starts "in high" and stops "in high."

IX. THE WEASEL

In wild life the race is not always to the swift, nor the battle to the strong. For instance, the weasel catches the rabbit and the red squirrel, both of which are much more fleet of foot than is he. The red squirrel can fairly fly through the tops of the trees, where the weasel would be entirely out of its element, and the rabbit can easily leave him behind, and yet the weasel captures and sucks the blood of both. Recently, when the ground was covered with our first snow, some men at work in a field near me heard a rabbit cry on the slope below them. Their dog rushed down and found a weasel holding a rabbit, which it released on the approach of the dog and took to the cover of a near-by stone wall. The whole story was written there on the snow. The bloodsucker had pursued the rabbit, pulling out tufts of fur for many yards and then had pulled it down.

Two neighbors of mine were hunting in the woods when they came upon a weasel chasing a red squirrel around the trunk of a big oak; round and round they went in a fury of flight and pursuit. The men stood and looked on. It soon became apparent that the weasel was going to get the squirrel, so they watched their chance and shot the bloodsucker. Why the squirrel did not take to the tree-tops, where the weasel probably would not have followed him, and thus make his escape—who knows? One of my neighbors, however, says he has seen where a weasel went up a tree and took a gray squirrel out of its nest and dropped it on the snow, then dragged it to cover and left it dead. The weasel seems to inspire such terror in its victim that it becomes fairly paralyzed and falls an easy prey. Those cruel, blazing, beadlike eyes, that gliding snakelike form, that fearless, fatelike pursuit and tenacity of purpose, all put a spell upon the pursued that soon renders it helpless. A weasel once pursued a hen to my very feet and seized it and would not let it go until I put my foot upon it and gripped it by the back of the neck with my hand. Its methods are a kind of *Schrecklichkeit* in the animal world. It is the incarnation of the devil among our lesser animals.

X. MISINTERPRETING NATURE

We are bound to misinterpret Nature if we start with the assumption that her methods are at all like our methods. We pick out our favorites among plants and animals, those that best suit our purposes. If we want wool from the sheep, we select the best-fleeced animals to breed from. If we want mutton, we act accordingly. If we want cows for quantity of milk, irrespective of quality, we select with that end in view; if we want butter-fat, we breed for that end, and so on. With our fruits and grains and vegetables we follow the same course. We go straight to our object with as little waste and delay as possible.

Not so with Nature. She is only solicitous of those qualities in her fruits and grains which best enable them to survive. In like manner she subordinates her wool and fur and milk to the same general purpose. Her one end is to increase and multiply. In a herd of wild cattle there will be no great milchers. In a band of mountain sheep there will be no prize fleeces. The wild fowl do not lay eggs for market.

Those powers and qualities are dominant in the wild creatures that are necessary for the survival of the species—strength, speed, sharpness of eye and ear, keenness of scent; all wait upon their survival value.

Our hawks could not survive without wing-power or great speed, but the crow survives without this power, because he is an omnivorous feeder and can thrive where the hawk would starve, and also because no bird of prey wants him, and, more than that, because he is dependent upon nothing that requires speed to secure. He is cunning and suspicious for reasons that are not obvious. The fox in this country requires both speed and cunning, but in South America Darwin saw a fox so indifferent and unafraid that he walked up to it and killed it with his geologist's hammer. Has it no enemies in that country?

Nature's course is always a roundabout one. Our petty economies are no concern of hers. Man wants specific results at once. Nature works slowly to general results. Her army is drilled only in battle. Her tools grow sharper in the using. The strength of her species is the strength of the obstacles they overcome. We misinterpret Darwin when we assume that Nature selects as man selects. Nature selects solely upon the principle of power of survival. Man selects upon the principle of utility. He wants some particular good—a race-horse, a draft-horse—better quality or greater quantity of this or that. Nature aims to fill the world with her progeny. Only power to win in the competition of life counts with her. As I have so often said, she plays one hand against the other. The stakes are hers whichever wins. Wheat and tares are all one to her. She pits one species of plant or animal against another—heads I win, tails you lose. Some plants spread both by seed and runners, this doubles their chances; they are kept in check because certain localities are unfavorable to them. I know a section of the country where a species of mint has completely usurped the pastures. It makes good bee pasturage, but poor cattle pasturage. Quack grass will run out other grass because it travels under ground in the root as well as above ground in the seed.

XI. NATURAL SCULPTURE

We may say that all the forms in the non-living world come by chance, or by the action of the undirected irrational physical forces, mechanical or mechanico-chemical. There are not two kinds of forces shaping the earth's surface, but the same forces are doing two kinds of work, piling up and pulling down—aggregating and accumulating, and separating and disintegrating.

It is to me an interesting fact that the striking and beautiful forms in inorganic nature are not as a rule the result of a building-up process, but of a pulling-down or degradation process. A natural bridge, an obelisk, caves, canals, the profile in the rocks, the architectural and monumental rock forms, such as those in the Grand Cañon and in the Garden of the Gods, are all the result of erosion. Water and other aerial forces are the builders and sculptors, and the nature and structure of the material determine the form. It is as if these striking forms were inherent in the rocks, waiting for the erosive forces to liberate them. The stratified rocks out of which they are carved were not laid down in forms that appeal to us, but layer upon layer, like the leaves of a book; neither has the crumpling and deformation of the earth's crust piled them up and folded them in a manner artistic and suggestive. Yet behold what the invisible workmen have carved out of them in the Grand Cañon! It looks as though titanic architects and sculptors had been busy here for ages. But only little grains of sand and a vast multitude of little drops of water, active through geologic ages, were the agents that wrought this stupendous spectacle. If the river could have builded something equally grand and beautiful with the material it took out of this chasm! But it could not—poetry at one end of the series and dull prose at the other. The deposition took the form of broad, featureless, uninteresting plains—material for a new series of stratified rocks, out of which other future Grand Cañons may be carved. Thus the gods of erosion are the artists, while the builders of the mountains are only ordinary workmen.

XI

RUMINATIONS

I. MAN A PART OF NATURE

This bit of nature which I call myself, and which I habitually think of as entirely apart from the nature by which I am surrounded, going its own way, crossing or defeating or using the forces of the nature external to it, is yet as strictly a part of the total energy we call nature as is each wave in the ocean, no matter how high it raises its crest, a part of the ocean. Our wills, our activities, go but a little way in separating us from the totality of things. Outside of the very limited sphere of what we call our spontaneous activities, we too are things and are shaped and ruled by forces that we know not of.

It is only in action, or in the act of living, that we view ourselves as distinct from nature. When we think, we see that we are a part of the world in which we live, as much so as the trees and the other animals are a part. Intellect unites what life separates. Our whole civilization is the separating of one thing from another and classifying and organizing them. We work ourselves away from rude Nature while we are absolutely dependent upon her for health and strength. We cease to be savages while we strive to retain the savage health and virility. We improve Nature while we make war upon her. We improve her for our own purposes. All the forces we use—wind, water, gravity, electricity—are still those of rude Nature. Is it not by gravity that the water rises to the top stories of our houses? Is it not by gravity that the aeroplane soars to the clouds? When the mammoth guns hurl a ton of iron twenty miles they pit the greater weight against the lesser. The lighter projectile goes, and the heavier gun stays. So the athlete hurls the hammer because he greatly outweighs it.

II. MARCUS AURELIUS ON DEATH

Marcus Aurelius speaks of death as "nothing else than a dissolution of the elements of which every human being is composed." May we say it is like a redistribution of the type after the page is printed? The type is unchanged, only the order of arrangement is broken up. In the death of the body the component elements—water, lime, iron, phosphorus, magnesia, and so on—remain the same, but their organization is changed. Is that all? Is this a true analogy? The meaning of the printed page, the idea embodied, is the main matter. Can this idea be said to exist independent of the type? Only in the mind that reads the page, and then not permanently. Then it is only an arrangement of molecules of matter in the brain, which is certainly only temporary. On the printed page it is a certain combination of white and black that moves the cells of the brain through the eye to create the idea. So the conception in our minds of our neighbor or friend—his character, his personality—exists after he is dead, but when our own brain ceases to function, where is it then?

We rather resent being summed up in this way in terms of physics, or even of psychology. Can you reconstruct the flower or the fruit from its ashes? Physics and biochemistry and psychology describe all men in the same terms; our component parts are all the same; but character, personality, mentality—do not these escape your analysis? and are they not also real?

III. THE INTERPRETER OF NATURE

Emerson quotes Bacon as saying that man is the minister and interpreter of Nature. But man has been very slow to see that he is a part of that same Nature of which he is the minister and interpreter. His interpretation is not complete until he has learned to interpret himself also. This he has done all unconsciously through his art, his literature, his religion, his philosophy. Painting interprets one phase of him, music another, poetry another, sculpture another, his civic orders another, his creeds and beliefs and superstitions another, so that at this day and age of the world he has been pretty well interpreted. But the final interpretation is as far off as ever, because the condition of man is not static, but dynamic. He is forever born anew into the world and experiences new wonder, new joy, new loves, new enthusiasms. Nature is infinite, and the soul of man is infinite, and the action and reaction between the two which gives us our culture and our civilization can never cease. When man thinks he is interpreting Nature, he is really interpreting himself—reading his own heart and mind through the forms and movements that surround him. In his art and his literature he bodies forth his own ideals; in his religion he gives the measure of his awe and reverence and his aspirations toward the perfect good; in his science he illustrates his capacity for logical order and for weighing evidence. There is no astronomy to the night prowler, there is no geology to the woodchuck or the ground mole, there is no biology to the dog or to the wolf, there is no botany to the cows and the sheep. All these sciences are creations of the mind of man; they are the order and the logic which he reads into Nature. Nature interprets man to himself. Her beauty, her sublimity, her harmony, her terror, are names which he gives to the emotions he experiences in her presence. The midnight skies sound the depths of his capacity for the emotion of grandeur and immensity, the summer landscape reveals to him his susceptibility to beauty.

It is considered sound rhetoric to speak of the statue as existing in the block of marble before the sculptor touches it. How easy to fall into such false analogies! Can we say that the music existed in the flute or in the violin before the musician touches them? The statue in the form of an idea or a conception exists in the mind of the sculptor, and he fashions the marble accordingly. Does the book exist in the pot of printer's ink? Living things exist in the germ, the oak in the acorn, the chick in the egg, but from the world of dead matter there is no resurrection or evolution. Life alone puts a particular stamp upon it. We may say that the snowflake exists in the cloud vapor because of the laws of crystallization, but the house does not exist in a thousand of brick in the same sense. It exists in the mind of the builder.

The sculptor does not interpret the marble; he interprets his own soul through the medium of the marble—the picture is not in the painter's color tubes waiting to be developed as the flower is in the bud; it is in the artist's imagination. The apple and the peach and the wheat and the corn exist in the soil potentially; life working through the laws of physics and chemistry draws their materials out and builds up the perfect fruit. To decipher, to interpret, to translate, are terms that apply to human things, and not to universal nature.

We do not interpret the stars when we form the constellations. The grouping of the stars in the heavens is accidental—the chair, the dipper, the harp, the huntsman, are our fabrications. Does Shelley interpret the skylark, or Wordsworth the cuckoo, or Bryant the bobolink, or Whitman the mockingbird and the thrush? Each interprets his own heart. Each poet's mind is the die or seal that gives the impression to this wax.

All the so-called laws of Nature are of our own creation. Out of an unfailing sequence of events we frame laws—the law of gravity, of chemical affinity, of magnetism, of electricity—and refer to them as if they had an objective reality, when they are only concepts in our own minds. Nature has no statute books and no legislators, though we habitually think of her processes under these symbols. Human laws can be annulled, but Nature's laws cannot. Her ways are irrevocable, though theology revokes or suspends them in its own behalf. It was Joshua's mind that stopped while he conquered his enemies, and not the sun.

The winds and the tides do not heed our prayers; fire and flood, famine and pestilence, are deaf to our appeals. One of the cardinal doctrines of Emerson was that all true prayers are self-answered—the spirit which the act of prayer begets in the suppliant is the answer. A heartfelt prayer for faith or courage or humility is already answered in the attitude of soul that devoutly asks it. We know that the official prayers in the churches for victory to the armies in the field are of no avail—and how absurd to expect them to be—but who shall say that the prayer of the soldier on the eve of battle may not steady his hand and clinch his courage? But the prayer for rain or for heat or cold, or for the stay of an epidemic, or for any material good, is as vain as to reach one's hands for the moon.

IV. ORIGINAL SOURCES

The writers who go directly to life and Nature for their material are, in every age, few compared with the great number that go to the libraries and lecture-halls, and sustain only a second-hand relation to the primary sources of inspiration. They cannot go directly to the fountain-head, but depend upon those who can and do. They are like those forms of vegetation, the mushrooms, that have no chlorophyll, and hence cannot get their food from the primary sources, the carbonic acid in the air; they must draw it from the remains of plants that did get it at first-hand from Nature. Chlorophyll is the miracle-worker of the vegetable world; it makes the solar power available for life. It is in direct and original relation to the sun. It also makes animal life possible. The plant can go to inorganic nature and through its chlorophyll can draw the sustenance from it. We must go to the plant, or to the animal that went to the plant, for our sustenance.

The secondary men go to books and creeds and institutions for their religion, but the original men, having the divine chlorophyll, go to Nature herself. The stars in their courses teach them. The earth inspires them.

V. THE COSMIC HARMONY

The order and the harmony of the Cosmos is not like that which man produces or aims to produce in his work—the order and harmony that will give him the best and the quickest results; but it is an astronomic order and harmony which flows inevitably from the circular movements and circular forms to which the Cosmos tends. Revolution and evolution are the two feet upon which creation goes. All natural forms strive for the spherical. The waves on the beach curve and roll and make the pebbles round. From the drops of rain and dew to the mighty celestial orbs one law prevails. Nature works to no special ends; she works to all ends; and her harmony results from her universality. The comets are apparently celestial outlaws, but they all have their periodic movements, and make their rounds on time. Collisions in the abysses of space, which undoubtedly take place, look like disharmonies and failures of order, as they undoubtedly are. What else can we call them? When a new star suddenly appears in the heavens, or an old one blazes up, and from a star of the tenth magnitude becomes one of the first, and then slowly grows dim again, there has been a celestial catastrophe, an astronomic accident on a cosmic scale. Had such things occurred frequently enough, would not the whole solar system have been finally wrecked, or could it even have begun? For the disharmonies in Nature we must look to the world of the living things, but even here the defeats and failures are the exception—else there would be no living world. Organic evolution reaches its goal despite the delays and suffering and its devious course. The inland stream finds its way to the sea at last, though its course double and redouble upon itself scores of times, and it travels ten miles to advance one. A drought that destroys animal and vegetable life, or a flood that sweeps it away, or a thunderbolt that shatters a living tree, are all disharmonies of Nature. In fact, one may say that disease, pestilence, famine, tornadoes, wars, and all forms of what we call evil are disharmonies, because their tendency is to defeat the orderly development of life.

The disharmonies in Nature in both the living and the non-living worlds tend to correct themselves. When Nature cannot make both ends meet, she diminishes her girth. If there is not food enough for her creatures, she lessens the number of mouths to be fed. A surplus of food, on the other hand, tends to multiply the mouths.

Man often introduces an element of disorder into Nature. His work in deforesting the land brings on floods and the opposite conditions of drought.

He destroys the natural checks and compensations.

VI. COSMIC RHYTHMS

The swells that beat upon the shores of the ocean are not merely the result of a local agitation of the waters. The pulse of the earth is in them. The pulse of the sun and the moon is in them. They are more cosmic than terrestrial. The earth wears her seas like a loose garment which the sun and moon constantly pluck at and shift from side to side. Only the ocean feels the tidal impulse, the heavenly influences. The great inland bodies of water are unresponsive to them—they are too small for the meshes of the solar and lunar net. Is it not equally true that only great souls are moved by the great fundamental questions of life? What a puzzle the tides must have been to early man! What proof they afford of the cosmic forces that play upon us at all times and hold us in their net! Without the proof they afford, we should not know how we are tied to the solar system. The lazy, reluctant waters—how they follow the sun and moon, "with fluid step," as Whitman says, "round the world"! The land feels the pull also and would follow if it could. But the mobile clouds go their way, and the aerial ocean makes no sign. The pull of the sun and the moon is upon you and me also, but we are all unconscious of it. We are bodies too slight to affect the beam of the huge scale.

VII. THE BEGINNINGS OF LIFE

It is remarkable, I think, that Professor Osborn, in his "Origin and Evolution of Life," makes no account of the micro-organisms or unicellular lives that are older than the continents, older than the Cambrian rocks, and that have survived unchanged even to our times. I saw in the Grand Cañon of the Colorado where they were laid down horizontally on the old Azoic or original rocks, as if by the hand of a mason building the foundation of a superstructure. All the vast series of limestone rocks are made up from the skeletons of minute living bodies. Other strata of rocks are made up of the skeletons of diatoms. Some of our polishing powders are made from these rocks. Formed of pure silex, these rocks are made up of the skeletons of organisms of many exquisite forms, *Foraminiferæ*. The Pyramids are said to be built of rocks formed by these organisms. "No single group of the animal kingdom," says Mr. W. B. Carpenter, "has contributed, or is at present contributing, so largely as has the *Foraminiferæ* to the formation of the earth's crust." In the face of these facts, how unsatisfactory seem Professor Osborn's statements that life probably originated on the continents, either in the moist crevices of rocks or soils, in the fresh waters of continental pools, or in the slightly saline waters of the "bordering primordial seas." This last suggestion comes nearer the mark. There is no variation during geologic time of these primordial living organisms. All conceivable changes of environment have passed over them, but they change not. Bacteria struggle together, one form devouring another form. Unicellular life long precedes multicellular. Biologists usually begin with the latter; the former are fixed; with the latter begins development or evolution, and the peopling of the world with myriads of animal forms.

VIII. SPENDTHRIFT NATURE

Emerson says, "Nature is a spendthrift, but takes the shortest way to her ends." She is like ourselves, she is ourselves written large—written in animal, in tree, in fruit, in flower. She is lavish of that of which she has the most. She is lavish of her leaves, but less so of her flowers, still less of her fruit, and less yet of her germinal parts. The production of seed is a costly process to the plant. Many trees yield fruit only every other year.

I say that Nature is a spendthrift only of what she has the most. Behold the clouds of pollen from the blooming pines and from the grasses in the meadow. She is less parsimonious with her winged seeds, such as of the maple and the elm, than with her heavy nuts—butternuts, hickory-nuts, acorns, beechnuts, and so on. All these depend upon the agency of the birds and squirrels to scatter them. She offers them the wage of the sweet kernel, and knows that they will scatter more than they eat. To all creatures that will sow the seeds of her berries she offers the delectable pulp: "Do this chore for me, and you will find the service its own reward." All the wild fruits of the fields and woods hold seeds that must be distributed by animal agency. Even the fiery arum or Indian turnip, tempts some birds to feast upon its red berries, and thus scatter the undigested seeds. The mice and the squirrels doubtless give them a wide berth, but in the crop of the fowl the seeds have the sting taken out of them. You cannot poison a hen with strychnine.

We ourselves are covetous of those things of which we have but few, extravagant with those of which we have an abundance. When the Western farmer burns corn in place of coal, be assured he sees his own account in it. We husband our white pine, and are free with our hemlock; we are stingy with our hickory, and open-handed with our beech and chestnut.

XII

NEW GLEANINGS IN FIELD AND WOOD

As I saunter through the fields and woods I discover new acts in Nature's drama. They are, however, the old acts, played again and again, which have hitherto escaped my notice, so absorbed have I been in the rise and fall of the curtain, and in the entrances and exits of the more familiar players. I count myself fortunate if, during each season, I detect a few new acts on the vast stage; and as long as I live I expect to cogitate and speculate on the old acts, and keep up my interest in the whole performance.

I. SUNRISE

The most impressive moment of the day here in the Catskills is the rising of the sun. From my cot on the porch I see the first flash of his coming. Before that I see his rays glint here and there through the forest trees which give a mane to the mountain crest. The dawn comes very gently. I am usually watching for it. As I gaze I gradually become conscious of a faint luminousness in the eastern sky. This slowly increases and changes to a deep saffron, and then in eight or ten minutes that fades into a light bluish tinge—the gold turns to silver. After some minutes the sky, just at the point where the sun is to appear, begins to glow again, as if the silver were getting warm; a minute or two more and the brow of the great god is above the horizon line. His mere brow, as I try to fix my eye upon it, fairly smites me blind. The brow is magnified by the eye into the whole face. One realizes in these few seconds how rapidly the old earth turns on its axis. You witness the miracle of the transition of the dawn into day. The day is born in a twinkling. Is it Browning who uses the word "boil" to describe this moment?—"Day boils at last." Gilder, I think, speaks of it as a scimitar flashing on the brim of the world. At any rate, I watch for it each morning as if I were seeing it for the first time. It is the critical moment of the day. You actually see the earth turning. Later in the day one does not note in the same way the sun climbing the heavens. The setting sun does not impress one, because it is usually enveloped in vapors. His day's work is done and he goes to his rest veiled and subdued. He is new in the morning and old at his going down. His gilding of the clouds at sunset is a token of a fair day on the morrow; his touching them with fire in the morning is a token of wind or storm. So much we make of these things, yet the sun knows them not. They are local and only earth phenomena, yet the benefaction of the sun is as if it shone for us alone. It is as great as if this were the case, and yet the fraction of his light and heat that actually falls upon this mote of a world adrift in sidereal space is so infinitely small that it could hardly be computed by numbers. In our religion we appropriate God to ourselves in the same way, but he knows us not in this private and particular way, though we are all sharers in the Universal Beneficence.

II. NATURE'S METHODS

Nature baffles us by methods so unlike our own. Man improves upon his inventions, he makes them better and better and discards the old. The first airplane flew a few miles with its pilot; now the airplane flies hundreds of miles and carries tons of weight. Nature has progressed steadily from lower to higher forms, but she keeps all her lower forms; her first rude sketches are as precious to her as the perfected models. There is no vacancy at the bottom of her series, as there is in the case of man. I am aware that we falsify her methods in contrasting them with those of man in any respect. She has no method in our sense of the term. She is action, and not thought, growth and not construction, is internal and not external. To try to explain her in terms of our own methods is like trying to describe the sphere in terms of angles and right lines.

The origin of species is as dark a problem as is the origin of the secondary rocks. What factors or forces entered into the production of the vast variety of stratified rocks, differing as widely from the original Adam rock, the granite, as the races of men differ from one another? There is just as much room for natural selection to work in one case as in the other. We find where two kinds of rock touch, one overlying the other, and absolute difference in texture and color, and no union between them. How account for their juxtaposition? Rock begat rock, undoubtedly, and the aerial forces played the chief part, but the origin of each kind is hidden in the abyss of geologic time, as is that of the animal species.

The position of the camel with reference to the giraffe in Africa is analogous to that, say, of the Catskill conglomerate to the laminated sandstone that lies beneath it. They are kindred; one graduates into the other. Whence the long neck and high withers of the giraffe? The need of high feeding, say the selectionists, but other browsing animals must have felt the same need. Our moose is strictly a browsing animal, and, while his neck and shoulders are high, and his lips long, they do not approach those of the giraffe. The ostrich has a long neck also, but it is a low feeder, mainly from the ground.

We can only account for man and other higher forms of life surviving in the highway of the physical forces on the ground that the wheels and tramping hoofs missed them much oftener than they hit them. They learned instinctively to avoid these destructive forces. Animal life was developed amid these dangers. The physical forces go their way as indifferent to life as is your automobile to the worms and beetles in the road. Pain and suffering are nothing to the Eternal; the only thing that concerns It is the survival of the fit, no matter how many fall or are crushed by the way; to It men are as cheap as fleas; and they have slaughtered one another in Europe of late without help or hindrance from the Eternal, as do the tribes of hostile ants. The wars of the microbes and the wars of men are all of a piece in the total scheme of things. The survivors owe their power of survival to the forces that sought their destruction; they are strong by what they have overcome; they graduated in that school. Hence it is that we can say that evil is for us as much as it is against us. Pain and suffering are guardian angels; they teach us what to shun.

How puzzling and contradictory Nature often is! How impossible, for instance, to reduce her use of horns to a single rule. In the deer and elk tribe the antlers seem purely secondary sexual characteristics. They are dropped as the season wanes; but the antelopes do not drop their horns, and in Africa they are singularly ornamental. But with our common sheep the horns are sexual manifestations; yet the old ram does not shed his horns. Nature will not be consistent.

Back in geologic time we had a ruminant with four horns, two on the nose and two on the crown, and they were real, permanent, bony growths.

What a powerful right fore limb Nature has given to the shovel-footed mole, while the chipmunk, who also burrows in the ground, has no special tool to aid him in building his mound of earth; he is compelled to use his soft, tender little nose as a pusher. When the soil which his feet have loosened has accumulated at the entrance to his hole, he shoves it back with his nose.

Even to some of her thistles Nature is partial. The Canada thistle sows its seeds upon the wind like the common native thistle; then in addition it sends a big root underground parallel with its surface, and just beyond the reach of the plough, which sends up shoots every six or seven inches, so that, like some other noxious weeds, it carries on its conquests like a powerful besieging army, both below ground and above.

A bachelor of laws in Michigan writes me in a rather peremptory manner, demanding an answer by return mail as to why robins are evenly distributed over the country instead of collected in large numbers in one locality; and if they breed in the South; and he insists that my answer be explicit, and not the mere statement "that it is natural law." I wonder that he did not put a special-delivery stamp on his letter. He is probably wondering why I am so dilatory in answering.

There seems to be an inherent tendency in nearly all living things to scatter, to seek new fields. They are obeying the first command—to increase and multiply. Then it is also a question of food, which is limited in every locality. Robins do not breed in flocks, but in pairs. Every gas is a vacuum to every other gas; and every locality is a vacuum to the different species of birds that breed there. The seed-eaters, the fruit-eaters, the insect-eaters, and the omnivorous feeders, like the robin—in other words, the sparrows, the flycatchers, the warblers—may and do all live together in harmony in the same narrow area.

The struggle of which we have heard so much since Darwin's time is mainly a natural sifting and distributing process, such as that going on all about us by the winds and the waters. The seeds carried by the winds do not thrive unless they chance to fall on suitable ground. All may be "fit" to survive and yet fail unless they are also lucky. What so frail as a spider's web, and yet how the spiders thrive! Nature gives the weak many advantages.

There is a slow, bloodless struggle of one species with another—the fleet with the slow, the cunning with the stupid, the sharp-eyed and sharp-eared with the dull of eye and ear, the keen of scent with the blunt of scent—which we call natural competition; but the slow, the stupid, the dull-eyed, dull-eared, and dull-scented find their place and thrive for all that. They are dull and slow because they do not need to be otherwise; the conditions of their lives do not require speed and sharpness. The porcupine has its barbed quills, the skunk its pungent secretion. All parts of nature dovetail together. The deer and the antelope kind have speed and sharp senses because their enemies have speed and sharp senses. The small birds are keen-eyed and watchful because the hawks are so, too. The red squirrel dominates the gray squirrel, which is above him in size and strength, and the chipmunk below him, but he does not exterminate either. The chipmunk burrows in the ground where the red cannot follow him, and he lays up a store of nuts and seeds which the red does not. The weasel easily dominates the rat, but the rat prospers in spite of cats and traps and weasels.

The sifting of species is done largely by environment, the wet, the cold, the heat—the fittest, or those best adapted to their environment, survive. For some obscure reason they have a fuller measure of life than those who fall by the way.

III. HEADS AND TAILS

I have heard a story of a young artist who, after painting a picture of a horse facing a storm, was not satisfied with it, and, feeling that something was wrong, asked Landseer to look at it. Instantly the great artist said to him, "Turn the horse around."

The cow turns her head to the storm, the horse turns his tail. Why this difference? Because each adopts the plan best suited to its needs and its anatomy. How much better suited is the broad, square head of the cow, with its heavy coating of hair and its ridge of bone that supports its horns, to face the storm than is the smooth, more nervous and sensitive head of the horse! What a contrast between their noses and their mode of grazing! The cow has no upper front teeth; she reaps the grass with the scythe of her tongue, while the horse bites it off and loves to bite the turf with it. The lip of the horse is mobile and sensitive. Then the bovine animals fight with their heads, and the equine with their heels. The horse is a hard and high kicker, the cow a feeble one in comparison. The horse will kick with both hind feet, the cow with only one. In fact, there is not much "kick" in her kind. The tail of the cow is of less protection to her than is that of the horse to him. Her great need of it is to fight flies, and, if attacked in the rear, it furnishes a good hold for her enemies. Then her bony stern, with its ridges and depressions and thin flanks, is less fit in any encounter with storm or with beast than is her head. On the other hand, the round, smooth, solid buttocks of the horse, with their huge masses of muscles, his smooth flanks, and his tail—an apron of long, straight, strong hair—are well designed to resist storm and cold. What animal is it in Job whose neck is clothed with thunder? With the horse, it is the hips that are so clothed. His tremendous drive is in his hips.

IV. AN UNSAVORY SUBJECT

If a rose by any other name would smell as sweet, I suppose the breath of the obscene fungus by any other name would smell as rank. The defensive weapon of our black-and-white wood pussy would probably not be less offensive if we called him by that name alone, instead of the common one by which he is universally known.

While in southern California last winter I heard of one that took up his abode in the basement of a house that stood on the side of a hill in the edge of the country. It was in a sort of lumber-room where all sorts of odds and ends had accumulated. On some shelves was a box of miscellaneous articles, such as lids to tin cans, bed castors, old toothbrushes, bits of broken crockery, pieces of wire, chips of wood, and the dried foot and leg of a hen. One morning, on opening the door of the basement, the mistress of the house was surprised to see the whole collection of trash laid out in a line across the floor. The articles were placed with some degree of regularity covering a space about fifteen inches wide and ten feet in length. There were sixty-one articles in the row.

Having such an unsavory creature in the basement of one's house is rather ticklish business; not so perilous as a stick of dynamite, yet fraught with unpleasant possibilities. They cleared away the exhibit and left the door open, hoping their uninvited guest would take his departure. But he did not. A few nights later he began another collection, finding a lot of new material—among other things a box with old atomizer bulbs, four of which bulbs he arranged here and there, in the row—a motley array.

What is his object? I confess I do not know. No one has seen him do it, as he works at night, but there is little doubt that it is his work.[3] The Western skunk is a small creature, not much bigger than a gray squirrel. He can hide behind a dustpan.

3 Later investigations point to this having been the work of a wood rat instead of a skunk.—C. B.

I wish some one would tell me why this night prowler so often seems to spray the midnight air with his essence which leaves no trace by day. He never taints his own fur with it. In the wilds our Eastern species is as free from odor as a squirrel or a woodchuck. Kill or disturb one by day or night in his haunts, and he leaves an odor on the ground that lasts for months. While at a friend's house in the Catskills last August a wood pussy came up behind the kitchen and dug in the garbage-heap. We saw him from the window in the early evening, and we smelled him. For some reason he betrayed his presence. Late that night I was awakened by a wave of his pungent odor; it fairly made my nose smart, yet in the morning no odor could be detected anywhere about the place. Of course the smell is much more pronounced in the damp night air than by day, yet this does not seem an adequate explanation. Does he signal at night to his fellows by his odor? He has no voice, so far as I know. I have never heard him make a vocal sound. When caught in a trap, or besieged by dogs in a stone wall, he manifests his displeasure by stamping his feet. He is the one American who does not hurry through life. I have no proof that he ever moves faster than a walk, or that by any sign, he ever experiences the feeling of fear, so common to nearly all our smaller animals. His track upon the snow is that of a creature at peace with all the world.

V. CHANCE IN ANIMAL LIFE

Chance plays a much larger part in the lives of some animals than of others. The frog and the toad lay hundreds of eggs, the fishes spawn thousands, but most birds lay only five or six eggs.

A spendthrift with one hand, Nature is often a miser with the other. She lets loose an army of worms upon the forests, and then sends an ichneumon-fly to check them. She wastes no perfume or color upon the flowers which depend upon the wind to scatter their pollen. Cross-fertilization is dear to her, and she invents many ingenious ways to bring it about, as in certain orchids. She will rob the bones of the fowl of their lime to perfect the shell of the egg. She wastes no wit or cunning on the porcupine or on the skunk, because she has already endowed each of them with a perfect means of defense.

Two things Nature is not chary of—fear and pain. She heaps the measure here because fear puts her creatures on the safe side; it saves them from many real dangers. What dangers have lurked for man and for most wild things in the dark! How silly seems the fear of the horse! a fluttering piece of paper may throw him in a panic. Pain, too, safeguards us; it shields us against real dangers. The pains of childbirth are probably no check upon offspring, because the ecstasy of procreation, especially on the part of the male, overcomes all other considerations.

VI. MOSQUITOES AND FLEAS

Mosquitoes for the North and mainly fleas and ticks for the South—this seems to be Nature's decree, at least in this country. The mosquitoes of the Far North pounce upon one suddenly and ferociously, while our Jersey mosquitoes hesitate and parley and make exasperating feints and passes. On the tundra of Alaska, if I stopped for a moment a swarm of these insects rose out of the grass as if they had been waiting for me all the years (as they had) and were so hungry that they could not stand upon the order of their proceeding, but came headlong.

In Jamaica the dogs were persecuted almost to death by the fleas. They were the most sorry, forlorn, and emaciated dogs I ever saw. Life was evidently a burden to them. I remember that Lewis and Clark, in their journey across the continent, were greatly pestered by fleas. I have found that our woodchucks, when they "hole up" in the fall, are full of fleas.

VII. THE CHANGE OF CLIMATE IN SOUTHERN CALIFORNIA

I have just been reading, for the third time, Dana's "Two Years Before the Mast," my sojourn near San Diego for a few months, where so many of the scenes and events he describes took place, having given me a renewed interest in the book.

It is very evident that the climate of southern California has greatly changed since Dana was here in the trading ships Pilgrim and Alert, in 1832 and 1833. The change has been from wet to dry. At that time his ship collected, and others engaged in the same trade collected, hundreds of thousands of hides and great quantities of tallow, all from cattle grown by the missions between San Diego and Santa Barbara. This fact implies good pasturage. The cattle grazed on the hills and plains that are now, during a large part of the year, as dry as a bone. At present cattle left to their own devices on this coast would soon starve to death.

Dana describes violent storms of wind and rain, mainly from the southeast, which the ship, anchored a few miles off the coast, or cruising up and down, experienced at all times of year—one or more storms each week, often lasting for days. One December he describes it as raining every hour for the whole month. The dread of the southeasters was ever present with the sailors. One of these, lasting three days, which came out of a cloudless sky, blew the sails to tatters. Nowadays a southeast storm of half a day is, according to my experience, an uncommon occurrence. To-day scarcely a drop of rain falls here from April till November, yet Dana describes many heavy rains in August. At present, in some of the interior valleys, where they grow alfalfa by means of irrigation, I see herds of well-kept dairy cows. In the season of rains the grass springs up and for a time cattle do well, but during the long dry season there is no pasturage save dry pasturage.

Although winter is supposed to be the rainy season here, I have been here during three seasons and have so far seen only light rains. To-day (December 16th) the earth is like powder as deep down as you care to dig. Yesterday I saw a man dragging in grain, and a great cloud of dust streamed out behind him. Ten or more years ago there was a very heavy rainfall in this locality that inundated large sections of the country and destroyed much property, the dry San Diego River getting out of bounds and carrying away bridges and floating houses on its banks. But it has been as dry as a highway ever since. It is clear that when the big rains do come they are more sporadic and uncertain than formerly.

VIII. ALL-SEEING NATURE

Sitting by a flat rock one summer morning, on my home acres in the Catskills, I noticed that the wild strawberry-vines sent out their runners over the rock, the surface of which is on a level with the turf, just as over the ground. Of course they could not take root, but they went through all the motions of taking root; the little clusters of leaves developed at intervals, the rootlets showed their points or stood at "attention," and the runners pushed out two or three feet over the barren surface and then seemed to hesitate like a traveler in the desert whose strength begins to fail. The first knot, or, one might say, the first encampment, was about one foot from the last one upon the turf, the next one about eight inches farther in; then the distance dropped to six inches, then to four. I think the runner finally gave it up and stopped reaching out. Each group of leaves apparently draws its main sustenance from the one next behind it, and when this one fails to reach the soil it loses heart and can give little succor to the next in front. The result is that the stools become smaller and smaller, and the distances between them less and less, down the whole line.

Nature's methods are seen in the little as well as in the big, and these little purple runners of the vine pushing out in all directions show the all-round-the-circle efforts of Nature as clearly as do the revolving orbs in sidereal space. Her living impulses go out in all directions. She scatters her seeds upon the barren as well as upon fertile spots. She sends rains and dews upon the sea as well as upon the land. She knows not our parsimony nor our prudence. We say she is blind, but without eyes she is all-seeing; only her creatures who live to particular ends, and are limited to particular spheres, have need of eyes. Nature has all time and all space and all ends. Delays and failure she knows not. If the runners of her strawberries do not reach their goal, the trouble corrects itself; they finally stop searching for it in that direction, and the impulse of the plant goes out stronger and fuller on other sides.

If the rains were especially designed to replenish our springs and supply our growing crops, the clouds might reasonably be expected to limit their benefactions, as do our sprinkling carts; but the rains are older than are we and our crops, and it is we who must adjust ourselves to them, not they to us.

The All-Seeing, then, has no need of our specialized vision. Does the blood need eyes to find its way to the heart and lungs? Does the wind need eyes to find the fertile spots upon which to drop its winged seeds? It drops them upon all spots, and each kind in due time finds its proper habitat, the highly specialized, such as those of the marsh plants, hitting their marks as surely as do others.

Our two eyes serve us well because our footsteps are numbered and must go in a particular direction, but the goal of all-seeing Nature is everywhere, and she arrives before she starts. She has no plan and no method, and she is not governed.

These conceptions express too little, not too much. Nature's movements are circular; her definite ends are enclosed in universal ends. The rains fall because the vapors rise. The rain is no more an end than is the rising vapor. Each is a part of the great circuit of beneficent and malevolent forces upon which our life (and all life) depends, upon which the making of the soil of the earth and the shaping of the landscape depend; all vegetable and animal life, all the bloom and perfume of the world, all the glory of cloud and sky, all the hazards of flood and storm, all the terror of torrents and inundations, are in this circuit of the waters from the sea to the sky, and back again through the rivers to the sea. In our geologic time there is, in this circuit of the waters, more that favors life than hinders it, else, as I so often say, we should not be here. The enormous destruction of human life, of all life, which has taken place and will continue to take place, in this beneficent circuit, is only an incident in the history of the globe; the physical forces are neither for nor against it; they are neutral; life to be here at all has to run these risks; has to run the gantlet of these forces, and to get many a lash and gash in the running. Against the suffering and death incident thereto there is no insurance save in the wit of man himself. All this wit has been developed and sharpened by much waste and suffering. We learn to deal with difficulties through the discipline of the difficulties themselves. If man were finally to learn to control the rains and the floods, it would be through the experience which they themselves bring him. The demons that destroy him are on his side when he strikes with the strength which they give him. Gravity, which so often crushes and overthrows him, is yet the source of all his might. The fire that consumes his towns and cities is yet the same fire that warms him and drives his engines across the continent.

There is no god that pities us or weeps over our sufferings, save the god in our own breasts. We have life on heroic terms. Nature does not baby us nor withhold from us the bitter cup. We take our chances with all other forms of life. Our special good fortune is that we are capable of a higher development, capable of profiting to a greater extent by experience, than are the lower forms of life. And here is the mystery that has no solution: we came out of the burning nebulæ just as our horse and dog, but why we are men and they are still horse and dog we owe to some Power, or, shall I say, to the chance working of a multitude of powers, that are beyond our ken. That some Being willed it, designed it, no; yet it was in some way provided for in the constitution of the world.

THE END

Ingram Content Group UK Ltd.
Milton Keynes UK
UKHW012016250523
422376UK00003B/19